Just Beyond the Shadows

Written by
J.J. Crane

Just Beyond the Shadows

Copyright © 2016 by J.J. Crane.

Acknowledgments

I want to thank my lovely wife for all her support. Others who have helped with suggestions and edits are LeeAnn W, John S, Wendy D, Lois L, Kim C, MaryAnn T, & Anna D.

You can contact me at jjcrane7@gmail.com
Please visit me on Facebook – JJ Crane, author

Cover Photo – iStock. by Getty Images

Also by JJ Crane – The Jersey Devil

Forward

I am neither a dissenter or true believer in Bigfoot. Rather, I am an optimistic skeptic. I believe there is the possibility for such a creature to exist and remain elusive.

For disclosure sake, I attended a BFRO event in Pennsylvania several years ago. I walked and photographed the area where the Jacobs sighting took place – I describe this sighting within the pages of this book. At this outing, I also participated in performing calls to see if we could produce any signs of Sasquatch. Nothing of note surfaced, though we did manage to stir up some owls who returned several of our calls. I did meet people who brought a lot of passion to the subject. It was interesting to see that believers in Bigfoot stretched the gamut of professions from pilots and doctors to mechanics and welders.

All characters and situations described in this book are fictional. Any resemblance to people or events is purely coincidental.

Chapter 1

"So how does it feel to finally be a free man?"

Chet Daniels didn't react to the prison guard's voice or the question. Not a muscle on his weary face moved as he stared down the long, gray-walled hallway before him. He had dreamt of being free, and now, on the precipice of his leaving the prison that entombed him for just over twelve years, he fell into a daze.

Chet flashed back to the first day he entered Oregon State Penitentiary. He vividly pictured the three officers who escorted him; two on either side and one in front. Chained at the ankles and wrists, the guards shoved him along with their nightsticks, jabbing him in the ribs, as they headed towards the general population wing of the prison. Chet could still hear them betting on when he would lose his virginity. Taking a deep breath, he let the vision fade.

"I don't think I've ever felt less sensation in my entire life," Chet finally answered as the two approached a steel door.

He had only interacted with the new guard, whose name he'd already forgotten, a handful of times in the recent past. The young man smiled too much for his type of work. Chet was relieved that he wouldn't have to watch years of anger, disappointment and worry chisel away at the poor guy as he had seen with others who worked in the prison system.

"Maybe some fresh air will do you good. Free air," the officer said before punching in a security code, then swiping a key card in the appropriate slot. A loud steel clack echoed around them, the locking device disengaging. "How does it feel to walk without chains on?"

Chet glanced down at his feet then his hands, clenching and curling them. He could still feel cold steel dig into his wrists and ankles. Relaxing his hands, holding them out in front of him, he realized it was the first time since entering this place that he did not have them on outside of general population. He wondered if this was why he felt so strange. He didn't bother looking at the young officer. Instead, he turned his attention to the next long, empty corridor that led towards another set of steel doors. Once through that last barrier, the next hallway would bring him to see the prison's psychiatrist for the last time.

After they passed through the second security door, Chet took several steps before he noticed the guard had stopped. He turned and looked back with a raised brow. The officer nodded. Chet grinned, realizing the young correctional officer was letting him walk the final steps unattended.

Walking down the straightaway that housed the offices for caseworkers and psychiatrists, he became keenly aware of the silence surrounding him, no chains clanging away. Without the aid of escorts, he nearly forgot which door to look for.

"Take it easy Chet. Nice and slow," he said to himself as began to concentrate on numbers. He wanted Room 11. Once, sometimes twice a week for nearly eight years he visited Dr. Drasner. Most of those visits occurred in his office. The doctor favored helping inmates feel less incarcerated by having them visit him, rather than meet in a gloomy gray sterile classroom within earshot and sight of the active prison area.

Chet counted the doors until he came to the one he needed. He grabbed the door handle and held it for a moment. He smiled. It was the first time he had grabbed this door handle on his own. Usually, an accompanying officer opened the door for him. He enjoyed the mild chill of the brushed steel's touch. Taking a deep breath, he turned the handle.

"Congratulations Chet," a veteran officer he knew by the name of Ol' Bob said. Ol' Bob had worked in the prison for over thirty years and was set to retire in a couple of months. "Make the best of it… at least long enough that I'll never see you here again."

Chet nodded, trying to conceal a grin. Ol' Bob's job was to sit with inmates in the doctor's waiting room and watch two monitors to make sure nothing suspicious or violent occurred during a session. Chet learned that some officers about to retire drew this post as their last assignment. Bob had been working this job for two years because of a leg injury he incurred breaking up a fight in 'the yard.' Ol' Bob both hated and loved the assignment. He read a lot, which he liked but it was also, at times, a painfully boring job. Chet noticed that Ol' Bob had put on some weight since getting the assignment. It didn't matter to Bob because his wife delighted in the fact that he was mostly safe at his present duties.

Chet sat down across from Ol' Bob. He crossed his legs, something he hadn't done in this room, ever. Instantly, the pangs of dehumanization flowed through him - his body shackled like some wild animal, hands clasped, legs bound by chains, never allowed to speak until given permission. During every humiliating moment he repeated to himself, *I am innocent.* He knew the truth, and would never take responsibility for the crime. Yet after twelve years of incarceration, he understood why the penal system process worked as it did. Why the system treated men as rabid beasts. He'd seen too many prisoners attack and even maim officers in fits of rage or worse, the pure joy of it. The security force trusted few if any inmates. In time, he accepted how many officers regarded him.

However, over time, Chet developed fair to good relations with some of the officers, a couple even believing in his innocence. After all, Chet didn't have an arrest record prior to his conviction. He was an Eagle Scout and an honors student in college. In his professional life, he worked as a writer for various outdoor magazines and websites reviewing camping and extreme wilderness gear. He was also in the process of writing about his research into the mysterious creature known as Bigfoot before his whole life came to a crashing halt. Now, just weeks' shy of his 39th birthday, all those adventures, memories and good times felt like they happened to another person in another life.

"Send him in," a voice crackled over the loudspeaker just above the two TV monitors.

Chet walked in feeling a bit off, not used to the freedom of opening a door or having someone keeping constant surveillance over him.

Dr. Drasner met Chet with a wide smile and open arms as he stepped from behind his cluttered desk. "Welcome, Chet. How does it feel on this first day or should I say hours of freedom?"

"It's nice not to have chains gripping my ankles or crushing my wrists," Chet said as he moved towards the fake leather chair he sat in when he visited Dr. Drasner.

Coming to the doctor's office acted as a kind of respite. He felt like a human being here despite the chains and orange jumpsuit he wore while visiting. The office felt more like a living room than a place of clinical study and review. Chet wondered if Dr. Drasner purposefully kept his office messy - folders and paperwork never had any rhyme or reason to their order. The books on the shelves that took up half the office walls always appeared pawed at and disorganized. Since inmates weren't allowed to touch anything while visiting, he speculated it was some kind of side research project on observational behavior.

"I'll let you know about the free part once I don't have to sleep here for a few nights," Chet said, settling into the chair.

Dr. Drasner nodded. "True. I believe you'll do fine. I understand you have family picking you up. That's good."

"My sister," Chet said. "One of the only people who really believed me."

Dr. Drasner's expression didn't shift from the poker face he often held when listening to inmates, a flat glare, the lines on his face steady, as if trained not to twitch, even subconsciously.

Chet knew the doctor's stare all too well, yet now, it didn't matter how he looked at him. "I'll bet she's already here in the receiving area."

"Any last thoughts you'd like to share?" the doctor asked leaning back in his chair more relaxed than Chet could ever recall seeing him. Usually, the doctor leaned forward wanting to capture every word, every nuance of a prisoner's delivery. "You know you have a court appointed psychiatrist to see for at least a year as you acclimate to freedom. Twelve years here is a long time. The world has changed... a lot."

"I don't have any doubt about that," Chet answered.

"How have you continued to shape your post-prison goals? We've talked about this."

Chet nodded. "I plan on getting back out to the only thing I know well, the wilderness."

"You're a good writer, an excellent writer in fact. I think you'll do well."

"An old friend at *Outside* magazine said he'd hook me up with some gear reviews to start me off. They want me to write under a pseudonym."

"You can see why?"

"I do," Chet said.

"How does that make you feel?"

Chet shrugged his shoulders with little care. "I'm getting a chance to pick up where I left off. The byline might be different, but the checks will have my name on it. Better than some of these other poor schmucks in here that have nothing to return to except getting back in here."

Dr. Drasner cracked a half smile. "No anger?"

"Anger?" Chet shot back somewhat surprised. "At the people giving me an opportunity? Not a chance. Hell, they're the ones making this whole thing bearable."

"But *you* have anger?"

Chet curled his lips as his eyes widened. "I've been telling you the same story for the last eight years I've seen you. It hasn't changed. I didn't kill those people. I was lucky to get out alive. I'm angry that I had to spend twelve years trying to fight off animals wanting to fuck me. Angry that the system screwed me harder than any of those other savages could," Chet said, his voice rising but not enough to garner any attention from Ol' Bob. "I know you want me to come to terms with my conviction, and in some ways, I have; I can thank you for that. But if you think I can just walk out of here and not carry some resentment, well then doc, you need to walk in my shoes for a bit because what you suggest ain't as easy as you might think."

Doctor Drasner sat up. "I never said it would be easy. I always suggested the more you could release that anger, not attach yourself to it, the freer of this place and your conviction you'll be."

Chet fell back in his chair blowing out a large exhale of air. "I know."

"You're a smart guy Chet. Keep your nose clean, you'll do fine. Get yourself as busy as you can so you can move forward. No one ever just lets the past go, but people learn how to balance and process it, not letting it weigh them down, suffocating them. Getting busy helps this process."

"Thank you doc, but let's face it, this thing will hang over me forever. I'll never shed the whispers or odd looks once someone realizes my past regardless of whether they believe me or not." Chet said.

"I'm not saying you're wrong. There isn't much you can do about how other people think but you have to handle it with dignity and always move forward," Dr. Drasner said.

"I know," Chet said with a nod. "But it would be best if I just disappeared. Started anew, anonymous somewhere, make up a past, like the government does for witness protection people."

"Yeah, well the government isn't going to do that for you," the doc said with a lighthearted quip.

Chet scanned the room again, wanted to ask about whether the books and paperwork were a contrived effort. Before the words came out, he smiled inside. *Better to let it be a mystery.* "I'll miss these sessions. It was the highlight of my stay."

Dr. Drasner stood up, reached his hand across the desk and gave Chet's hand a firm shake. "You're going to be fine. See the doctor a couple times a month for starters. Good luck out there. I'll keep an eye out for your work in the magazine." The doctor held his grip as if there was more to say.

"What?" Chet asked, noticing the doctor's prolonged look.

"Any chance you'll get back into searching for Sasquatch?"

Chet could sense the doctor wanted to ask the question. He had asked it less over the last year. He couldn't rightly remember the last time. Chet smirked, his head bobbing a little as if on a stiff spring. "It's not on my immediate radar." He took a deep breath. "Would you go out looking for Bigfoot if you knew the truth?"

Chapter 2

"I can't fuckin' believe you found this," Harlan McDaniel said, a mile-wide grin stretching across his round face. He pulled a tissue out of a box and wiped the perspiration beading on his forehead as he gazed at the small video cassette. "This is one of those digital tape formats before they went to discs and compact flash cards."

"I just hope there's footage," Jack Morrow said while pulling up a chair in Harlan's cramped, home office edit suite. "Can you play it?"

Harlan paused, his eyes searching his mind. "I may have a player. These tapes haven't seen use for at least decade or so. Stores and studios were giving this shit away when cameras began converting to CD's and DVD's."

"That fits the timeline perfect then," Jack said, opening a bottled water and taking a sip.

"You know what this can mean for Bigfoot research?" Harlan asked, his voice notching up in pitch.

"And what it could mean for Chet," Jack said having to remind Harlan of the railroading the now cult-like figure received by the courts.

Harlan stood up, only half hearing what Jack said while walking to a closet, opening it, revealing stacks of metallic boxes, all colored in shades of gray. Harlan's head bobbed back and forth, looking with purposeful intent, moving items to one side or another. He then dropped to one knee and began moving his hands through more cases, banging the old casings against each other without much care.

"Let me check another place," Harlan said. "I have stuff in my basement. You're probably in luck since I don't throw out much. Unlike my pristine surroundings," he said spreading his arms out, proud of how neat and orderly he kept his work area, "the basement is a hoarder's wet dream."

Jack didn't want to sit; he was too anxious. He stood up as Harlan exited the room. Glancing around, he did notice that Harlan kept a neat office. Aside from a pile of papers with notes scribbled on them next to the keyboard, the office itself, containing a deep brown wooden desk with two large 27-inch monitors on it, had little in clutter. Two walls contained shelves neatly organized with software and video editing books, DVD's of client videos, and external hard drives, all scored with black marker. A small glass top table just behind Harlan's workstation had a couple of magazines on it and two chairs for clients to sit at. Harlan's chair, a big fat black cushy leather piece of furniture that looked expensive, sat right in front of his desk. Jack also noticed that Harlan kept equipment out of immediate eyesight. Only a printer perched on a small stand near the table with the magazines was in immediate view, all the computer towers and accessories hid behind ventilated doors. Wires remained neatly tucked, hardly visible. A small card reader sat on the desk with the black wire running to the rear of the monitors and disappearing behind them.

"Got it, and an adapter," Harlan said holding a medium sized gray metal box. He dropped into his big chair and swung himself over to the far side of his desk, placing the metal box on it. He pulled out a VGA and two RF chords and began making connections to equipment inside the cabinet on his desk. "This should work just fine. Thankfully the playback deck was right out in the open as if it was waiting for me to come and get it."

When Harlan finished making the connections, he plugged the box in and powered it up.

Jack saw the lights on the deck turn on. "Success?"

"So far," Harlan answered without looking back as he went

to his mouse and keyboard and started calling up menus. "Have to find the auxiliary ports and see if the computer can pick it up."

"Why wouldn't it?" Jack asked.

"It should, but we're talking about ancient stuff in technology terms. As long as the two systems can speak to each other, we should be fine. By the time this technology was coming into play, editing systems had already gone more computer oriented. If this were ancient tape, like ¾ or beta, I'd have to go old school with converters and adapters I probably don't have on hand." Harlan stopped talking, realizing that old editing jargon wouldn't mean much to Jack. After a few taps on the keyboard, he looked up at the monitors. "Okay baby, we're in business. Let's see what this tape has on it."

Jack handed over the small cassette. Harlan gave it another once over. The casing didn't have any cracks. He released the protective plastic strip to examine the tape and aside from a couple of faint creases, it looked good. He tested the tension with his finger in the rollers and it seemed fine. Next, he placed the tape in the deck, shut the covering and hit play. Using the mouse, he began to navigate through the tape via his computer. He only saw black and no sound.

"Not looking good my friend," Harlan quipped staring at his screens.

"Wait a minute… did you rewind it?" Jack asked.

Harlan turned back towards him. He shook his head, his face serious until a big smile broke his stoic disposition. "Captain Obvious. Very good. How stupid of me. Let's go back in time and see what's what."

They both sat hoping for the best as Harlan rewound the tape at a slow rate. Snippets of broken footage flashed on the screen, but the signal on the tape did not allow it to transfer into anything discernible.

"Lots of drop out frames," Harlan said as he adjusted the pace to see if running the tape at a faster speed might somehow help grab a better video signal. He stopped the tape and turned to Jack. "I say we rewind it and start at the beginning. A fast rewind will give the tape some tension it may need."

"Couldn't that break the tape?" Jack asked.

Harlan shrugged. "Listen, you found this in an Oregon forest. The fact that we have anything at all is a miracle. Can it snap, yeah, I'm not going to lie, but we've been watching this thing, and all we've gotten are dropouts and no sound. It's rare but sometimes putting tension on tape can help. It's the best I can offer if we want any real shot at viewing this footage. If this is, what you think it is… this will be one of the most groundbreaking pieces of Bigfoot evidence the world has ever witnessed."

"That's what I'm hoping for," Jack said.

"It could prove that guy… what's his name… Chet's innocence."

Jack bit his tongue. He wanted to lash out but knew it would do no good. Jack knew his belief in Chet's innocence was more zealous than the average Sasquatch enthusiast. "Yeah, exactly, Chet Daniels."

"That's right, sorry," Harlan said. "You'd think I'd remember his last name as it's close to mine."

"Let's rewind the tape," Jack said rubbing his hands nervously together wanting to ignore his friend's apparent ignorance to the importance of what this could mean for Chet.

Harlan swung his chair around. "Done."

"Done?"

"Yeah, I rewound while we were talking. Took it upon myself to do that."

Jack's jaw dropped, horror stretching across his face. "Did it break?"

"No," Harlan answered with cool assuredness. "And you might want to close that stunned trap before flies get in there." Harlan turned back to the screen. "It's ready to go."

Jack brushed off his comment. "Hit play, smartass. Let's do it."

Broadcast Bars appeared, and both expressed joy at seeing the multi-colored array of rectangles, knowing that something survived. Then a long even tone sounded.

Harlan punched his fist to the ceiling. "We have audio," he shouted.

The bars stopped, then black, followed quickly by video footage. It was dark, but they could both make out the shapes of trees. They watched the footage brighten a little.

"Looks like someone hit the gain," Harlan said. "Technical thing you could do to most video cameras before ISO settings became a thing."

The footage revealed a campsite, tents; three visible to the camera before it turned and showed a fire. Several people sat around it.

"This is the area. I remember this clearing," Jack said as he pointed at the screen.

"You gonna record us having drinks," said a voice just outside the *camera's range.*

"Gotta document the whole damn thing. You never know. We get famous, you want this shit on tape," the cameraman said.

"That's Paul Jorgenson the cameraman speaking," Jack said.

The camera panned around settling on two women, late twenties, sitting on the far side of the fire from the camera's point of view. They put up their hands not wanting to speak to the camera.

Jack nodded with excitement. "Okay, that's Melanie Stansfield, the cute one. I think her and Chet had a thing going on, but that may simply be a rumor. The pudgier one, still attractive, is Stacey Wright. They both participated in a number of Sasquatch expeditions. I did meet Stacey once when I first got involved in looking for Bigfoot. She was friendly. From all accounts, both of them took the research very seriously."

The camera then panned to the leader of the group, Hollis Denneson, a Dutch immigrant who came over to the United States as a teenager. Hollis's father was an anthropologist who taught ancient cultures at the University of Oregon. Hollis became fascinated with tales of Sasquatch shortly after his father began to study Native American Cultures of the Northwest. Hollis was a tall man, nearly six foot five, skinny, with thinning blonde hair pulled back into a short ponytail. The camera also revealed another man, more familiar to both Jack and Harlan, Chet Daniels. When Chet caught the camera pointing at him, he smiled a placating grin, waved then went back to paying attention to Hollis who was talking about the evening's goals.

A few seconds of black followed before the footage reappeared following the crew as they broke camp to set up for the night's research. Jack and Harlan could hear the participants talking about meeting back at base camp shortly before sunrise. The members checked their walkie-talkies and went over the protocol for how they would exchange calls and wood knocks throughout the night.

The tape then went into a span of lots of dropouts in both video and audio. When the footage picked back up, Harlan and Jack could barely see the shapes of people moving about in the dark. Occasionally the footage recorded some snippets of conversation over the walkie-talkies but nothing of note. Video continued to come and go; audio popped and crackled to both of their dismay. Harlan spotted where the tape was in the spool. Shaking his head, he told Jack the tape was close to where it was when they put it in the deck.

"You think if you rewind it again, it might add more tension and help it out?" Jack asked.

"It's a faint possibility, but honestly, it appears like this is where the tape is damaged, and no amount of rewinding is going to save the footage."

"Then let's just keep watching. Even if there's a couple more seconds of something, it might be worth it."

"It's already worth something," Harlan shot back, turning his chair to look directly at Jack. "You've got footage of these people in the last hours of their lives. If anything, you have enough to make one hell of a documentary about their investigation and the murders."

"Killings," Jack answered with a straight firm tone. "Chet didn't murder those people."

Harlan raised his eyebrows, and toned down his response. He held some reservations about Chet's innocence. "He certainly paid the price. Twelve years is a long time... a short time for someone convicted of killing all those people."

"He barely escaped with his life. It must have been a nightmare up there," Jack said.

"And twelve years in prison isn't exactly living the dream," Harlan added.

Jack nodded. "Without a doubt... but the time has passed, and he should be getting out of jail anytime."

"How old is Chet now?"

Jack had to think. He knew the case well, followed it, and believed every word Chet offered even if the police and prosecution found Chet's story highly suspicious. However, without any tangible evidence, just circumstantial, Chet received a fifteen to twenty-year sentence. An appeal knocked the time back to just short of fourteen years. Good behavior earned an earlier release, but Jack couldn't remember the exact date of that.

"I'm pretty certain he's about forty, somewhere in there," Jack, answered. "I'd have to look it up to be precise."

Harlan turned his chair back to the monitors. "Hey, look at this," he said sitting up straight.

Footage returned. The camera pointed through the silhouette of several tall trees to reveal shades of red and orange color in the distant sky. A moment later a voice on the tape exclaimed how beautiful the sight was. A couple ooo's and ahh's rose up out of the quiet. Someone said it was still twenty minutes until sunrise. Again, the footage dropped out.

"Damn it," Jack shouted, grabbing the arms of the chair and giving them a quick shake. But, before his frustration could grow, the video reappeared. This time, the camera pointed at Hollis who was in mid-sentence. "*... the night was mostly silent but in the last hour, just after we all met up here at base camp we began to hear some howls. They were amazing. At first, we thought wolves, but it was more guttural and full. Chet gave a 'whoop' call, and several return calls came back. In all honesty, it's been rather creepy to have heard so many calls. They seem to be coming from all around us and closing in.*"

"He looks nervous," Harlan said.

Jack sat closer to the edge of his chair. "He does. Even the camera guy is jittery. Notice how the camera has a shake to it?"

The footage continued. Hollis turned away from the camera, and Paul began to widen the view, panning the camera around revealing the site. The clearing didn't look big, maybe fifty feet round at most, with a couple good-sized lichen and moss covered boulders protruding from the ground. Tall Douglas Firs shot straight up along the edge of the clearing, their silhouettes acting like giant prison bars surrounding the place.

"*Holy shit,*" a voice cried out off camera. "*A rock just missed me.*"

The camera panned over to Brandon Leaky, a distant cousin to the famous paleoanthropologist. Noticing the camera pointing at him, he gestured towards where the rock came from.

"Oh crap, another one," a girl shouted.

The camera swung over towards Melanie. She too pointed but with less composure. Shivering, she leaned against one of the boulders in a squatting, quasi-fetal position.

"Man, she looks like she has the shit scared out of her," Harlan said.

"Shit," Jack shouted. "Go back, go back."

"What, what?" Harlan asked.

"I thought I saw a rock come from out of the woods and cut through a portion of the screen."

Harlan rewound the scene back past Melanie pointing towards the woods.

"Okay, it should happen at any time," Jack said in a deliberate way, eyes glued to the monitor. "There it is. Did you see it?"

"Maybe," Harlan said. "Let me rewind again."

Harlan moved the video at a slow rate, almost frame by frame. He didn't want to miss it.

"There, upper left," Jack said scooting his chair closer to Harlan's, his finger pointing as far as it would reach.

"Got it," Harlan half shouted. "That's a pretty good size rock."

"Can we determine how big it is?" Jack asked.

"I'm sure, but I don't know the math in how to do that. But I'd guess it's the size of a football," Harlan said. "Maybe a little smaller."

"Whoa, if that hits ya, you'd know it," Jack said.

"Let's see what it does," Harlan said letting the video play at normal speed.

Almost immediately Melanie shouted that a rock flew by, hitting the ground just a few feet away from them. Paul began to pan the camera when a scream cut through the air so loud and shrill it crunched the audio. Harlan and Jack watched as the camera jerked around in search for the source of the scream. When the camera finally settled, it found Stacey, on her knees, holding the side of her face. Blood streamed between her fingers covering a portion of her ear and right temple area. Chet and Hollis came to her aid. They asked her what happened. Crying, she said a rock hit her. Hollis pulled a bandage from one of the cargo pockets in his pants and began to put pressure on the wound. Another bloodcurdling scream shrieked followed by a man's yell of horror. The camera turned towards the cries. Melanie and Brandon clung to each other, frozen; the two couldn't pry their eyes off the woods in front of them.

"What happened?" Paul asked.

"In there, I swear I saw two large Bigfoot," Melanie said. Brandon nodded in approval.

"Where?" Paul asked, positioning himself to point the camera towards the woods while using the two witnesses for an over the shoulder shot.

"In there," Brandon said, pointing straight at three tall trees distinctly close to each other compared to the more spread out growth. "Right in that grouping."

Then Melanie screamed, tears suddenly streaming down her face, spit flying out of her mouth as she fell to her knees. "There it is. Oh my God, there's the other one. What's happening? Why are they here?"

Paul's camera jerked trying to locate what she was pointing at. He zoomed in to search.

"Oh my God," Jack gasped. "There's one of them."

The camera bobbed a little bit before settling in on the object of their horror. A creature, standing nearly eight feet tall, with wide rounded shoulders stood out from the deep shadows of the woods behind it. Dark hair covered its entire body except for portions of the face, which had a dark gray leathery aspect to it. Jack and Harlan could see the creature's nose resembled a conflation of human and ape, its round eyes set back in the skull reminded them what computer animations portrayed Neanderthals to appear like.

They heard Paul, the cameraman, gasp. The camera jerked, audible nervous panting followed before the picture finally steadied. A moment later, another creature appeared from out of the shadows as if fading into the scene. Paul reacted to it the same time as Jack and Harlan.

"HOLY Shit," Harlan shouted. "You see those two, they are huge."

"See them? I nearly friggin' wet myself when the second one appeared," Jack said.

Harlan and Jack watched as the camera held firm zooming into the two beings standing stoically, like carved totem poles. Neither could tell if the creatures were breathing. They began to fixate on the eyes: darkness surrounded by a milky white. Even more disturbing, the beings didn't blink.

Stacey began screaming at the figures from off camera. She shouted for them to go away. The beasts didn't react to her voice.

Another scream caused Paul to jerk the camera. This time, it was Melanie. Hollis soon began yelling, but in a panicked fashion, the voice cracking with tears. The camera turned again, seemingly not sure what to focus on when a gunshot sounded. The camera swept past Melanie who now lay on the ground in a fetal position, twitching with fear. The camera then spotted three new large creatures between seven and nine feet tall. They walked out of the woods and into the opening. Paul cursed with fright but kept the camera rolling.

Another shot exploded then another. Paul settled his camera and captured a round piercing one of the Bigfoot in the shoulder. The beast flinched as if merely punched then roared a low guttural, bone vibrating growl bearing its yellow and gray teeth, revealing two distinct canines. All three creatures moved deeper into the clearing.

Jack and Harlan listened as more voices screamed, some pleading mercy, others yelling in tortured panic. They watched the camera turn, almost as if Paul was about to run into the woods. After several steps, a wall of a creature filled the frame. Paul winced. A second later, the camera pointed straight up through the tops of the trees before crashing to the ground. Everything on the tape went black.

Chapter 3

"Understood… thank you, I'll see you Monday morning 10 am," Chet said, his voice emotionless as he hung up the phone.

"Another glass of water?" Chet's sister Janice asked. She stood just to the side of the old dark gray leather recliner Chet sat in. She half wanted to weep staring at her brother's drawn, weary face, a smile once vibrant now seemingly buried by years of pain and anger. She always loved his bright blue eyes, so alive with the next adventure. Now, she saw a man, sullen, quiet, traces of gray streaking through his once thick brown hair.

Chet didn't answer right away. Noticing his own silence, he broke his distant gaze into nothingness and looked up at Janice. "Yes, water sounds good."

Janice ran a hand through his disheveled hair. "It's okay now. Take your time. If you can't sleep tonight, just watch some TV, rent a movie, or go on the computer, but I want you to know you are safe here… always welcome. I love you." She leaned over and kissed his head.

Chet squeezed her arm with appreciation. "Well starting Monday, it all gets real. That was my probation officer. My new best friend."

"Listen," Janice said as she walked back towards her kitchen. "I have mail for you when you're ready for that. I also have lots of e-mails for you as well. They're all stored on the Cloud. I'll show you how to access them."

"The Cloud?"

"Sorry," she said with a chuckle. "Yeah, it's all new stuff. The kids had to show me how to use it. It isn't hard."

Chet let out an audible exhale. "I got a lot of catching up to do."

Janice came back with the water. "You'll get up to speed. I know you. You aren't going to let any moss grow under your feet. You'll get busy again, like before… I know it." She wondered, though, seeing her brother slumped into the chair.

Chet smiled and picked up a copy of *Outside Magazine* from the small table next to his chair. He took in a breath thinking how much he enjoyed writing for the periodical before he went to prison. It was a matter of time before he'd be back to writing for them again. This time, however, under a pseudonym.

"You see," she said. "You're getting the game going."

The cheap black rectangular digital clock on the dresser in Chet's room glowed 2:20 am. The red numbers looked hazy as he turned his heavy eyes back to the computer. His sister set up their old tower system and nineteen-inch flat screen monitor in the guest room knowing Chet would want to research and write. Janice's husband, Robert Fortney, an airline pilot, assembled a prefab desk that fit perfectly into a corner of the room.

Chet leaned back in his chair, rubbing his eyes. He finally felt tired, exhausted even. It felt good. For nearly three hours, he read stories about himself online. He found a number of Bigfoot sites, blogs, and Facebook pages and read all the wildly different takes about him and his case. Chet couldn't believe the chatter; let alone learning about a television show, *Science and Sasquatch*, where a crew of researchers looked for the mysterious creature hosted by an old acquaintance, Sam Ashford. He chuckled. "Figures. If anyone could pull off getting a TV show, Sam could."

Chet spent much of the computer time simply shaking his head in amazement at how little people actually knew about his case. The suppositions people made and felt compelled to express, no matter how off course, stunned him. Little of it elicited any anger or joy. He appreciated the supportive voices. The ones that carried vitriol towards him, he just let those roll off his back. After twelve years in jail dealing with that zoo, trying to avoid getting shanked, or screwed - the online noise was a walk in the park.

Chet awoke just shy of ten in the morning. Fully clothed, he lay on top of the bed covers. He couldn't remember going to bed. It didn't matter. He wasn't in jail. He stared at the ceiling for a couple minutes. He smiled, fully realizing this was the first time in twelve years that the ceiling to the room he slept in wasn't some shade of life sucking gray. Another minute later, he heard the stampeding sound of feet barreling towards his room from the other side of the closed door. Voices of excited children followed. He heard Janice, trying not to yell, telling the kids to quiet down; "Uncle Chet might still be sleeping."

He walked downstairs. Janice had a fresh pot of coffee brewed, and she poured him a cup as soon as she saw him.

"The kids are up," Chet said with a touch of sarcastic obviousness.

Janice smiled wide. "I see someone's coming around. Sleep well?"

Chet nodded as Janice slid a hot cup of black coffee in front of him. "Slept hard," he said, stretching his eyes, trying not to yawn as wide as his mouth wanted.

"Good. Any plans for today or you haven't thought that far?"

"I don't know… what's today… Saturday?" He paused; froze in place. He'd been so regimented into a routine, the thought of being able to do anything paralyzed him. "I… I have no idea what I want to do."

Janice could see his confusion. "Why don't you go for a hike? Take the bike to one of the trailheads. You know the area. Believe me; Sandy, Oregon hasn't changed much. The trails, the woods, they're the same for the most part. I took the kids a couple of weeks ago and walked a few of the easier trails with them. It's a beautiful day, go out and enjoy."

Chet ran his tongue across his teeth. He felt perspiration on the back of his neck as anxiety rushed through his body. He kept his poise, but a tight demeanor gave away his true composure.

Janice placed a hand on Chet's shoulder. "It can't be easy. I can't even fathom what you must be feeling or thinking, but you're home. You need to step out at some point. Better sooner than later. I don't want to be a pain in the ass about it, but I'm also the one that's going to kick your ass to get you moving. You can live life now. What happened, happened, there's no denying it, but it's over, you have this moment in time," she said with an exaggerated pointing gesture. "And God willing tomorrow and many more."

Chet tilted his head, stuck his tongue into his cheek and stared at his sister. "What'd you and the shrink get together to read the same script?"

Janice grinned then gave a short laugh. "If you can't do the woods, then go for a bike ride."

Chet nodded. He knew his sister was right. He looked out the big bay window that overlooked a view of Mount Hood. Not a cloud littered the sky, and he could see the snowcapped peak. He knew there were a lot of woods between him and the top of that mountain, not that he was going to scale it any time soon but he knew the woods would call. They always did.

Chapter 4

The drone of crickets offered Corrine Beltner the white noise needed to settle down while trying to relax in her tent. A fairly experienced outdoorswoman, she didn't care for bushwhacking trips. Corrine hiked and camped along many of the well-known trails of the popular parks in Northern California and Oregon. Bushwhacking (the art of hiking without using trails) never interested her much. She had done a few over the years to say she had, but it wasn't her forte'. Now, laying in her tent, staring straight up into the orange vinyl, she found herself roughly fifteen miles from the nearest marked trail. It bothered her. She was out of her comfort zone and for Corrine, safety, preparation and confidence played an important role in successful camping in the northwest corridor of the United States. If for nothing else, a bear could easily overrun a campsite and no one in the real world would know for weeks, if ever.

It was late, just after midnight. She wondered if she had taken on too much just to impress her latest boyfriend, Kyle Marks, an expert outdoorsman who had explored areas of the northwest he believed no other person ever laid eyes on. She didn't doubt it. Kyle scaled most of the highest peaks in Canada and the United States. Kyle also spent six months solo hiking from the north end of Gifford Pinchot National Forest in Washington all the way to Modoc National Forest and emerging south of Mount Shasta. Kyle bragged that he only hiked trails for a quarter of the trip, opting to bushwhack with a compass and map. He had the pictures to prove it and even published a book titled, *21st Century Explorer.* It became something of a Holy Grail for extreme hikers and in turn, he became something of a cult celebrity.

Corrine admitted that his renown, as well as his tall, athletic frame, blazing green eyes and wavy surfer like blonde hair played a huge role in her crush. They met at an expo in

Portland showcasing outdoor gear. He represented a top line company that manufactured and sold tents and other camping equipment. In fact, the orange tube-like tent she laid in was one of the manufacturers, lent out for Kyle to test and review. What she admired about Kyle was his passion. Unlike other pitchmen, Kyle didn't pull a snake oil salesman act by overzealously pitching the manufacturer's products. He did what good salespersons do, sell themselves, share his experience with the gear and develop a trust with the client. He listened to customers; let them talk, while he asked questions about them and their needs. She knew the craft because she did sales for hospital supplies and always performed in the top five of twenty on her team.

After initially meeting Kyle at the convention, she circled the floor a few times catching his glances on several occasions. Every time their eyes met, he tossed her an engaging smile, nothing overt, just a corner of the mouth grin acknowledging the contact. Towards the closing of that day, Corrine circled around one last time, this time with the aim to have a conversation. Kyle was ready and wanting. They chatted easily until the lights began to shut off then took their talk to a nearby pub where they chatted until closing. Happy with how the evening went, they exchanged numbers.

Corrine continued to stare into the orange. They now had dated six months. This was their first off trail adventure. She told him she wasn't comfortable with the whole idea; she enjoyed the outdoors, but risk taking wasn't high on her agenda. Kyle enjoyed the several hiking and camping trails they did together, but he yearned for something that offered more of a rush. He wanted to share his passion with her on going it alone in the wilderness. For their first time, he promised her nothing overly extreme, and they would go with another couple, Rob, and Teresa, to ease her nerves. She didn't know them, only heard about them through camping stories. Corrine acquiesced. Yet now, she couldn't sleep, her nerves wound high. She didn't want to alarm Kyle or the other couple to her anxiety, so she simply excused herself as having a headache and wanted to get some sleep to fight it off. She had to suck it up. It was only two more days; the weather forecast looked perfect and the hiking, though bushwhacking, appeared far from daunting. Kyle explained the whole trip. He took into account her trepidation and plotted out a solid wilderness trip that avoided anything dangerous. She appreciated the effort, but she couldn't shake the nerves.

In the midst of her racing thoughts, Corrine suddenly noticed something; the white noise of the forest's critters had ceased. She sat up, arms stiff, hands planted into the tent's flooring. Her eye's shifted around as if hoping they would entice her ears to hear better. Then another observation came to her; the others had stopped talking. Only silence filled the void of the world outside. Her heart began to pound. She could feel it beat against her sternum.

Taking a deep breath, she leaned forward to unzip the tent when it opened in front of her. Corrine fell back. She wanted to yell, but her voice became paralyzed.

Kyle put his finger up to his mouth then mouthed, 'I'm sorry.' He glanced back over his shoulder then back into the tent. He gestured with his finger for Corrine to follow him.

"What's wrong?" she said with the faintest whisper.

"Not sure," he said.

Corrine maneuvered herself out of the tent like a cat stalking prey. The light coming off the fire barely illuminated much beyond their pitched tents. A wall of darkness swallowed the area beyond them.

"Why's it so quiet?" she whispered into Kyle's ear as he guided her closer to the fire-pit.

"We thought we heard steps," Kyle said as quiet as he could.

"Bear?"

He shook his head.

"What then?"

He didn't answer. He just stared ahead, his eyes examining the darkness before him.

Corrine turned and could see the other couple standing perfectly still, their backs to her. Her skin crawled, the hairs on her arms rose with the feeling that something was now hunting them. Looking towards the fire, she could see it dwindling. If it went out or became nothing more than embers, then darkness would consume them. She could not let that happen. She bent down, grabbed a few branches piled to the side and placed them on the fire. The disturbance of new fuel caused a few crackles and sparks to fly. Looking up, she could see several eyes glaring at her as if she gave away their position in some kind of secret military maneuver. What surprised her most was Kyle's wild expression, his mouth agape breathing heavy, eyes wide, body movements stiff and deliberate. It was the first time she ever glimpsed fear in the man who had roamed the northwest alone for months. Standing, she took two steps so her body brushed the side of his.

"See anything?" she asked again in the quietest whisper.

"Not sure... but something is out there," Kyle answered.

"How do you know?"

Kyle bit his lip, blinked a couple times as if trying to find the right words. "Something or someone threw rocks at us shortly after we noticed everything went quiet."

Adrenaline rushed through Corrine. She felt herself sway into Kyle's body. She tried hiding her increasingly rapid breathing. "Rocks?"

He nodded while keeping his eyes trained on the darkness in front of him.

"Shit!" cried out Rob Haskins.

Corrine and Kyle turned, seeing Rob down on a knee facing towards the fire, his hand holding the side of his face.

Corrine, certified in first aid, moved towards him. "Are you all right?"

Rob looked up towards her, and she could instantly see small streams of blood trickling between his fingers. Corrine touched his hand and pulled it away to get a better look.

"It's a gash just below your temple. Not terrible, certainly not needing stitches but it does need a bandage," Corrine said.

"Another one," Kyle yelled as a rock hit the ground where Corrine had stood, bounced into the fire, kicking up embers. "What the hell!"

Teresa Sanders, Rob's longtime girlfriend, ducked into their tent then emerged holding a rifle. Corrine could see her breathing heavy, trying her best to remain calm. Rob brought the rifle along. Someone always brought a weapon on longer bushwhack hikes into the wilderness of the northwest.

"Be careful with that," Kyle said.

"Careful?" she questioned, panting, her hands wrapped tight around the weapon. "Whatever... whoever is out there is lucky I don't just start shooting."

"Give me the weapon," Kyle said as he signaled with his hand for her to give it over.

Rob stood up seeing the fright in Teresa's face. Placing his hand around the barrel, she gladly let it go into his hands.

"Enough of this shit," Rob said, a thin streak of blood still streaming down the side of his face. He brought the rifle up into a firing position, aimed it into the darkness and began a slow pan with the weapon. "I'll fire," he yelled. "I have enough ammo to make sure I hit one of you bastards."

Corrine made her way back to Kyle. She grabbed his bicep, her nails pinching into his flesh. Kyle didn't flinch at the pressure; he just kept scanning the area.

Their campsite began to lighten. The clouds that had covered most of the sky started to clear, revealing a setting moon that eked out enough light to define the shapes of the trees just thirty feet from the center of the fire pit.

"You see anything?" Kyle asked as a general question.

Rob still had the rifle at the ready. "Nothing yet."

"Over there," Corrine shouted out, pointing to where they all had entered into the clearing earlier in the day.

"I see it," Kyle shouted as he squinted trying to see a tall nebulous shape moving just beyond the shadows of the tree line before vanishing into the dark.

"What the hell is that?" Teresa asked, also having seen the shape.

"That's no bear," Rob said lowering the barrel of the rifle halfway.

"You think that's..." Kyle said not finishing his thought.

"What?" Corrine asked before catching herself. "No... you think?"

Teresa felt a presence and turned to look behind her. Immediately, she felt all the blood drain from her face. She screamed, mouth wide, terror-stricken.

They all turned and saw a behemoth of a creature, hairy, rust dark, nearly nine feet tall, raise its mammoth arms into the air before arching its head towards them and belted out a deep, vibration-bone rattling roar.

Corrine felt her gums throb as she stood petrified before a creature that could easily kill her with one hard swat of its giant hand.

Rob felt his kidney's squeeze, a trickle of urine escaping. The guttural baritone howl swarmed over them for several long seconds. It wasn't until they all closed their eyes as a way of shielding themselves that the numbing shriek ended. Opening their eyes, they caught a glance of the beast disappear into the forest.

Frozen, all the four of them could do was look at each other in disbelief. No one spoke. No one moved except to study their surroundings. It wasn't until the critters of the woods resumed their nightly chatter that the four of them finally began to relax.

Corrine waited for someone to speak but no one did. She wondered if they all fell under some kind of spell. Glancing around, the forest remained as if nothing had occurred, yet they all knew something very strange and unique just happened. She turned to the fire, the glowing embers and small flickering flames looked to gain a second life. A chill came over her, and she bent down to get closer to the heat. Teresa followed suit but said nothing. Corrine looked up to see the two men move about, surveying the landscape. The moon began to drop behind the trees allowing darkness to once again fill the area.

"What the hell just happened?" Teresa said to Corrine. She gazed at Corrine like a little girl who just lost her puppy.

Corrine barely shook her head. "I don't know."

"I want to leave," Teresa said.

"So do I," Corrine answered.

"At first light," Kyle said, overhearing them. He continued to stare in the direction the howling beast took off towards. "It's too dark now. There isn't enough moonlight for a safe exit, and I don't want to use just headlamps." He glanced at his watch. "Two hours… then we'll break camp and head out."

"In the meantime?" Teresa asked.

"In the meantime, Kyle and I will keep watch. You two make sure the fire stays up. There's enough wood for that," Rob said, not looking at them, just staring into the night.

The stars hadn't faded from the sky before the tents and sleeping bags found themselves neatly folded into their respective backpacks. The mostly extinguished fire smoldered and wisps of smoke floated into the air. Kyle made sure to kick plenty of dirt on it and even used some of his water to douse as much of the embers as he could. It was the shoddiest he ever left a wilderness camp. Kyle said if they hiked at a crisp rate with few breaks, they might make it back to Rob's truck by nightfall. Corrine had no doubt they would. She'd jog. She encouraged it for areas that opened up or revealed level surfaces. They all agreed some jogging would get them out of the forest quicker where appropriate. No one worried about expending too much energy, not after what they all just experienced.

Chapter 5

"I want to go back to that clearing where the attack took place," Jack said to the five gathered members of his Bigfoot expedition team. Jack explained he wanted to document a return to where the controversial Chet Daniels Sasquatch Attack took place in Willamette Forest. He not only wanted to prove Chet's innocence but once and for all, prove the existence of Bigfoot.

Jack went through Chet's case with the group. Though they had all heard or read something about it, Jack wanted to set the record straight as far as he believed it. He explained that an entire team of Bigfoot researchers disappeared with only Chet escaping. The story made national headlines. Police and the Forest Service combed the region for weeks. They didn't find any trace of the team and Chet's story seemed too farcical for anyone to take seriously.

Some members asked Jack if the authorities discovered any evidence of Sasquatch. He said a couple anonymous sources reported hearing strange calls, one even thinking they saw a giant figure run off into the thick of the woods. However, none of those stories made it into any official reports.

In time, the authorities charged Chet with the disappearance of all eight members of the expedition. Chet pleaded not guilty and repeatedly claimed his innocence. The prosecution had no true evidence worthy of linking Chet to killing any of them - no hair samples, blood stains, except for a scraping of blood found in Chet's index finger. Analysis couldn't determine if it belonged to anyone else's from the team. No clothing, gear or even the shotgun Chet claimed to have fired turned up in the search.

Jack described how Chet could not afford strong legal representation, and no legitimate law firm would touch the case since he claimed that a group of Sasquatch attacked his expedition team. Instead, he had to settle for a court-appointed lawyer. If it wasn't for the fact that the authorities didn't find a single body, Chet might have spent the rest of his life behind bars.

For the newbies in Jack's group, Chet's case gave them a moment of pause. Yes, they believed in Bigfoot, but something about the subject matter always allowed them to consider it a safe adventure. What Jack described was anything but safe. For the veteran researchers, they nodded, having heard and developed their own opinions about the case – most believing Chet's story to varying degrees.

"You say you have visited the site where the attack took place, why go back?" Avery Helmsly questioned. Avery, the oldest member in the room and a long time researcher, claimed to have had two Bigfoot sightings. The more prolific encounter occurred at night, at a camp he pitched while hiking for a week near the east end of Swift Reservoir, south of Mount St. Helens. He claimed his dog, Roger, a German Shepherd, woke him up with a low rumble of a growl. Avery thought it was a bear. He took out the short barreled shotgun he hiked with when soloing, slowly unzipped the tent, barrel pointing out. On the opposite side of his campsite, about twenty feet away, he saw an enormous bipedal creature nosing around the fringes of his small clearing. A three-quarter moon, on a clear night, illuminated enough that he could easily make out the shape of the creature that he guessed was seven feet tall. Dark hair covered its entire body, and it stood on its legs as natural as any person with just the faintest slouch in the shoulders. Avery said he sat mesmerized as the beast looked around picking at objects on the ground, not seeming interested in the smoldering fire or his tent. When Roger's growl grew louder, the creature stared straight at the tent. Avery said he locked in on solid eye contact with the creature. It held for a minute, just looking at Avery as if he was nothing more than a harmless inconvenience. Roger barked, and the creature turned and ran, disappearing from the scene in a flash, hardly making a sound as it vanished into the forest. Avery jumped out of his tent to see if he could locate the creature, but it was gone.

"You ask why go back? I'll tell you... it's because of this." Jack reached over to the TV stand and picked up a DVD. He displayed it like a child would at Show & Tell.

"What do you have there?" Amy asked. Amy Childs, a lightly tattooed Goth girl (a flying angel tat on the back of her left shoulder, a sunflower on the ankle and the words Live and Love on her left arm), with dark hair, and piercings in her mouth tongue, ears, nose and belly button, made a reputation as something of a Bigfoot groupie.

An eager worker well versed in videography, audio, and note taking, Amy also liked to share her tent with other attendees of such events. The particular sex didn't matter if the attraction sparked. Rumors had it that she bedded every research leader, male or female, married, engaged, taken or single that she went out into the woods with. Her best features often fell in the shadows of her lesser ones. Some investigators felt she gave their aims a bad name in a realm of investigation that already struggled for legitimacy.

Jack had slept with Amy on a number of occasions. He gave her a wink as he snapped the DVD from its case. They both had an understanding about unattached, casual sex. Both of them had this odd feeling that when their bodies gave way to age, they would probably settle down together. Jack never gave credence that Amy's presence brought a bad name to an expedition. In a mutual admiration, Amy reciprocated by becoming one of Jack's strongest supporters and his hardest worker.

Jack knelt and inserted the DVD. In seconds, broadcast

bars filled his 57-inch TV. "I think you will all find this highly enlightening."

The room fell silent as the footage began to play. Jack watched facial expressions, the slight jerk of a mouth, tightening of jaws, eyes widening. He noted pupils opening and closing, but no one took their eyes off the screen or made a sound; only the noise of the terror-stricken victims bounced off the walls in Jack's living room. When the screen faded to black, shoulders slumped, bodies fell back into their seats, heads shook in dismay, and big gasping breaths sounded.

"Where the… I mean how…" Zachary Jacobs stammered. Zachary, a professional outdoorsman, and guide throughout Oregon, Washington, and northern California.

Zachary wasn't the only one in the room floored by the footage they just witnessed. Stan Garner and Carl Turk sat back on the couch, silent, mouths agape. Carl ran his big hands over his bushy reddish goatee trying to absorb the video while Stan planted two fingers over his mouth like he was going to glue them into place.

Jack knew he had a lot of explaining to do. The footage he showed was a game changer. "To answer the big question, I hiked to the scene of the crime with another Squatcher some of you know, Pacer Bradford. We discovered several other similar clearings just off the search grid the police used."

"What?" Avery said half stunned, half excited at the prospect of an expedition to the region.

Jack smiled. He knew he had their attention, like fish to a tasty hooked worm. He pulled out a folded map he had by the television. "Pacer and I went over as many of the transcripts we could get our hands on dealing with the location of Chet's expedition in the mountains on the southern end of Hill Creek Lake. We believe he misremembered certain details in what he told police."

"Are you saying Chet lied to hide his guilt?" Carl asked. He knew of the case but didn't have a particular opinion on it.

"No, not at all," Jack said. "I think the trauma of the incident shuffled the deck on his memory. I believe he fell under the influence of those who may have coerced him into searching in the wrong areas. Let's face it; out there in the deep woods of Oregon, bushwhacking, it's not hard to get off track. You can be great with a compass and map but that doesn't mean just because you came to a small clearing, it's the exact clearing you think it is."

"You think the police may have gone to the wrong grouping of clearings?" Amy asked.

"Yes, I think it's possible," Jack said. "I think what's more apparent is that the authorities spent too much time combing areas east of the actual locations of the expedition."

"But from what I have read about the case, the authorities covered a greater area than just what Chet led them to," Avery said.

"Yes they did," Jack concurred, pointing at red dashed lines on the map. "But if you look at the search area, their circle is right on the border from where I believe the expedition actually pitched camp," Jack said as he pointed to black 'X's' he believed represented the expedition's actual campsites.

"And how do you know this?" Avery asked.

Jack grinned. "Because Pacer is a cousin of the former girlfriend of the cameraman, Paul Jorgenson, who shot this footage. About seven years after the expedition's disappearance, the girlfriend, Paula, became engaged to another guy. Pacer went over to help clear things out of her condo she shared with Paul and came across a box. In the box were materials from the planning of the expedition's trip including a marked-up map of the group's intended destination." Jack again pointed to the location on his map.

"As you can see, the expedition planned for the group to go just a touch west of the search zone." He could see others had questions. "Why Chet led authorities to the wrong location is a mystery I can't speak for. Remember, the authorities didn't allow him to go out and comb the area with them. There's a tremendous difference between pointing to something on a map and actually being on the ground and seeing the terrain. Chet didn't have the chance to go and say — *hey, this isn't where we were.*"

"It's hard for me to believe that Chet gets the location that wrong," Amy said. "From all I've read about him and in talking to others who knew him, he was a pretty knowledgeable outdoorsman." Others nodded turning to see what Jack would say.

"I understand," Jack said. "I've hiked the area. These clearings essentially all look alike. Ten, twenty to fifty feet of clearance, circular in shape, they all have rocks covering most of the openings. Plus, the terrain is rugged. You have to do some serious climbing and bushwhacking to get to these sites. Unless he lied, which I don't think he did. He either pointed to the wrong area on the map or those in charge missed the proper search area. But after reviewing Paul's notes, it appears the police concentrated on the wrong area. How else do you explain the video?"

People took a moment to ponder Jack's offering.

"Which begs the question of how you found this footage?" Zachary asked.

"Yes," Jack said knowing he'd have to answer the question. "The source of that footage came off an old digital tape before DVD, CD's and CF and SD cards."

"And you found it out there?" Stan asked with a wary expression. "Twelve years later, countless feet of rain, let alone snow, ice and other weather and you found usable footage?" Stan became more unconvinced of Jack's story as he spoke, the circumstances just too wild to comprehend.

Jack nodded and simply said, yes.

"How?" Carl asked, his point of view sliding over to support Stan's. "I mean, you have to go through this again. It just seems too implausible."

"Such an inquisitive group, that's why I love you guys," Jack said as he moved towards a small filing cabinet. Opening the top drawer, he reached in and retrieved a portion of an old video camera. Dark weathering stains and flakes of lichen still adorned it. "This my friends, is the camera Paul Jorgenson used to video capture the attack; an old Cannon over the shoulder ENG (electronic news gathering). In its day, it was the workhorse for in-the-field news gathering; a sturdily built piece of equipment, better than today's POS's. I found it lodged in a downed tree near the edge of a clearing. And before you ask how that came about, I'll confess, if it wasn't for the fact that I had to pee and walked off to the side to tend to business, I probably would never have found it. I was simply looking around when I caught a glimpse of something that had more shine to it than should among decomposing tree parts in a forest. At first, I had no idea that this was *thee* camera. As I walked back towards Pacer who was tending to a fire for the night, I realized the possibility of what I was holding. I wanted to head back home right then, but there was no way we were making it down the mountain unless we walked all night, a proposition neither of us found enticing."

"That must have been a hell of a sleepless night," Zachary interjected.

"Indeed. We scoured the area with even greater intensity," Jack continued. "Pacer had a small metal detector. We searched most of the night as a way to keep ourselves occupied."

"Did you find anything?" Amy asked.

Jack nodded. "Two buttons. Both different, found in the same clearing, about twenty feet apart. One came off a field jacket, either Chet's, Brandon's or Hollis's is my guess. The other is smaller, more decorative. Pacer has them. He had to cancel coming here last minute, but we think it came off one of the women's jackets."

"Wait a minute," Avery said waving his arms. A look of confusion and angst squeezed at his face as he tried to make sense of the news. "If you have all this, why didn't you bring it to the authorities? This can clear Chet. Besides that, the footage is clear evidence that a group of Sasquatch hunted down a group of humans. This footage is more important to Bigfoot research than all the pictures and fuzzy video ever assembled. Why have you waited?"

"Precisely because it is Bigfoot footage," Jack said, his voice easy. "We aren't talking about research that garners a whole lot of credibility. For one, the footage is shaky, dark, and has dropouts. What you saw was an edited and condensed version. There is very little in clear-cut evidence that this is Bigfoot or a family of them. You know right off that there are going to be detractors - loud ones. Every skeptic is going to try to debunk the footage and a whole host of others are going to believe in those debunkers."

"What are you talking about?" Carl barked. "We just saw it with our own eyes."

"Exactly," Jack said. "Bigfoot believer's eyes. Any skeptic will consider the source and look at it as tainted. We can't just come running out of the mountains saying look we have proof. It didn't work for Paterson,* and that's about the best footage ever to appear."

Avery stood up, his emotions both angry and perplexed. "Your footage can't remain amongst us as some trophy find. The authorities have to see this."

---

*- Patterson-Gimlin film depicts a walking Bigfoot alongside Bluff Creek in northern California. Filmed in 1967 it is considered one of the best pieces of evidence for confirming Bigfoot. The film is highly controversial with many who think the film is a hoax, while others contend the events on the film could not be faked.

"And they will," Jack said. "In good time. First I want to bring this to Chet and let him see it and see what he wants to do. I just learned yesterday that he is now a free man."

Not everyone in the group realized that Chet had left prison the week before. Also, Jack and Pacer's expedition and retrieval of the camera had only happened a month earlier. With this new information, the group better understood the logic in waiting before getting the authorities involved.

"I want to embark on a major expedition to the area," Jack continued. "Recreate their search while doing our own. The night vision equipment we have now is far better than anything they had back then," Jack said.

"You want Chet to participate?" Amy asked.

Jack nodded. "And he will."

Carl and Avery brushed off Jack's assumption. "I wouldn't count on it," Carl said.

"He will. He'll do it to clear his name," Jack said.

Amy nodded. She believed Jack. She believed Chet, deep down, wanted to exonerate himself. She had read nearly every interview and watched every video about him. Chet never wavered on his innocence. Chet took several polygraph tests, all of them proving that Chet believed in his innocence. Body language experts all expressed that Chet revealed no lies, no hidden motives, or cover-ups.

Zachary stood up. "What about seeing if Sam Ashford will join us? He's well versed in Chet's case."

All eyes snapped to Zachary who had worked with Sam in the past as a guide. Sam Ashford hosted a popular cult-like show, *Science and Sasquatch*. He led groups into Bigfoot hotspots and filmed the investigations. Some thought Sam as a self-serving attention grabber while others recognized him as a legitimate investigator who also happened to wisely parlay his passion into a money making television show. Regardless of one's opinion, Sam brought the Bigfoot subject more into the public discussion.

"Do you think you can get him?" Jack asked, liking the idea. He had met Sam twice but didn't have a relationship with him.

"I can reach out to him," Zachary said. "I don't know what kind of contractual obligations he has or whether Chet would agree to him coming along. If I can't reach him, I know a guy some of you have met or worked with in the past, Alex Redford. For those who don't recognize the name, he's the top moderator on the mother of all Bigfoot websites, *The Bigfoot Research Society*. I know he can get in contact with Sam."

"I know Alex as well; let's go that route," Jack said. "Right now we have neither individual, so let's just see what we can put together."

Chapter 6

Chet worked hard not to visit any Bigfoot websites or blogs after an initial flurry of reading about himself. Still, late at night, sitting at the computer in his room, he'd hover the cursor over links, his finger quivering like an addict looking for a fix. He had resisted temptation many times - until this night. His resolve began to wane as he held a glass of scotch in his hand.

Earlier in the day, he met with his parole officer, Janet Holloway for the second time in a week. Janet outlined the details of his parole for the coming weeks and months. Chet couldn't remember everything she said. His head swirled with the surrealism of what he had to endure, random drug tests, a series of reports and evaluations, community service obligations. He never accepted guilt for what happened to his team and wouldn't own it, ever. He felt terrible about the loss of life, but he wasn't guilty for their deaths and refused to kowtow to feeling like a criminal.

"Freedom my ass," he said, his right pointing finger still hovering above the mouse. With that sentiment, he let gravity drop his finger onto the left side of the mouse. He applied light pressure to the plastic and heard the little click.

The web page opened up to *The Bigfoot Research Society*, a collection of evidence, articles and home to the largest catalog of Bigfoot reports collected on the net. Its dominant blue background color and tree brown fonts hadn't changed since he last viewed the page right before his trial. The menu system hadn't changed much either, but the images displayed on the Home page all looked newer. He chuckled seeing a big banner ad for Sam Ashford's television show. Chet still couldn't believe that Sam worked his way into making Bigfoot expeditions into a reality television program, *Science and Sasquatch*.

"Good for him," Chet said aloud, with a half laugh. "Why not?"

Chet worked with Sam a couple of times when Sam first came onto the scene as an energetic and charismatic personality who ardently wanted to find a Sasquatch. Sam also came from money - not filthy rich money but enough that he could contribute significant funds to projects. There was a catch to his funding; he became a lead on the expedition. He wanted some say into how things happened. This aspect didn't play well with many. Folks thought he should cut his teeth like the rest of them and work his way up the ladder. He rubbed the more sensitive of those in the Bigfoot community the wrong way. Chet admitted he didn't care for Sam's bravado and should show some deference to the more veteran researchers. However, after getting to know Sam a bit, he liked him. Chet saw a genuine passion and honesty that he came to respect.

Chet glanced around at his options on the site and eyed the buttons for the forum and reports. He was curious to see what the discussion about his release had to offer, but something within him wavered from venturing there. He knew negativity awaited. After spending an afternoon of being reminded, he still had to fulfill parole obligations or take the chance of returning to jail, he didn't want to read anything that might rile him. With one glass of scotch already in him and another in his hand, he opted for Bigfoot sighting reports from across the country. *Safe*.

Chet glimpsed over the listing of states. Bigfoot sightings took place in nearly every state and Provence in Canada. The only difference... frequency. The northwest United States and British Columbia garnered the most attention. New reports constantly filled those pages. The moderators who managed the site, painstakingly went over every detail of the filed reports to tender them a grade. The grades reflected the degree of believability/authenticity among the moderators.

Reports receiving a D or Incomplete, echoed caution, meaning either there were questions about the credibility of the report, not enough information or if elements about the report had plausible explanations as something other than Bigfoot.

When submitting reports, Chet knew people were apt to mistake strange noises for Bigfoot. Calls by bears, wolves, coyote, fox, bobcats, elk, certain birds and mountain lions could often find themselves mistaken as Sasquatch sounds if not knowledgeable about such creatures. Chet also knew the work behind the grading. He helped develop the criteria before the website became as big as it did.

Grades garnering an 'A' rating had to include at least two critical criteria: One, a detailed account of the location for verification purposes. Two, some form of documentation. Accepted documentation included physical evidence - footprint or body imprint casts and/or pictures of the same. Also considered were pictures or video of tree structures (a unique bending, stacking, piling or constructed design using trees or other brush or forest growth). Lastly, any video of a Sasquatch that had no plausible explanation or photographs meeting the same criteria. Audio samples could help warrant an 'A' grade, but could not act as a stand-alone element. As Chet knew, 'A' grades happened infrequently.

More often, reports with lesser verifiable evidence (but still deemed plausible) received B grades. C grades were given to stories whose elements had a degree of credibility, but no proof to back them up. The vast majority of reports on the site garnered 'C' grades.

Rather than delve into the complicated world of reports in the northwest, Chet clicked Oklahoma. The southeastern region of that state had become something of a hotbed for activity, especially in the region of Hochatown State Park and extending up into the Ouachita Mountains. Chet went there for an outing, north of the park closer to Mountain Fork, the waterway that merged with Broken Bow Lake to its south. Chet found both the environment, evidence and the stories compelling enough to support a family of Bigfoot.

Chet glanced at the titles of the reports, and their accompanying grades - most garnered C's, second, B's, scattered D's and I's. He had to scroll down quite a bit to see an 'A.' He clicked that report, and up came several large images of footprints discovered on the outskirts of a farm bordering woods that led into thick hill country. The ensuing casts made, revealed a foot size of about a 29. As bonus, the report also included video of a Bigfoot Tree Structure, discovered two miles from where the footprints were found. These structures came in various forms. The one pictured, featured several trees bent into shapes representing something along the lines of a teepee or lean-to. Some theories suggested the structures acted as territory markers, and in some cases, possibly even shelter. Opening up a separate tab, he scanned a map of the state. Remembering his visit to Oklahoma, the location of the report looked about an hour northeast of where he had investigated. He didn't doubt Sasquatch roamed that remote region of the state.

Chet soon moved onto Ohio and New York. Though these two states contained less action, the activity they did have, clustered in spot specific areas. After a brief glimpse through some C and B reports, nothing of note grabbed him, so he then clicked onto Pennsylvania. Right off, he spotted a couple 'A' reports. All the reports centered in an area of north-central Pennsylvania (Allegheny National Forest) known for the Jacob's sighting. A hunter, Rick Jacob's set up a trail cam to prospect an area for hunting. What he discovered in reviewing the images were two pictures of a creature in an odd position that appeared more like a hairy primate trying its hand at a downward dog yoga pose. Dissenters argued the creature was a young, malnourished or diseased bear scavenging the ground for food. Bigfoot enthusiasts claimed the camera caught images of a young Bigfoot. Either way, the pictures caused quite a controversy.

No one could prove the creature in the image wasn't a Bigfoot because no one could prove that it was a bear or a person faking a pose. Chet never visited the region but knew several people who did. He learned the area was a hotbed for Bigfoot stories and given what he had found out about the terrain of the region; it offered plenty of space and food to support a Bigfoot grouping.

Taking another sip of his drink, then a second, he decided to return to the region he knew best, the northwest. Without hesitation, he clicked the link. The page loaded and he watched as a myriad of reports lined up. The reports listed with 'C' and 'B' grades dominated. As he scrolled, he came to an 'A' with an asterisk. He looked at the date; it occurred six weeks before his release from prison.

He read the report. He read it twice, then a third time. He felt himself go flush and lightheaded. He pushed back from the desk to catch his breath. With his heart pounding, Chet began to take deep breaths to slow down his anxiety. He wanted to scream out but didn't. He felt tears roll down his cheeks. Looking at his shaking hands, he noticed the glass of scotch a foot out of reach. He pulled himself back towards the desk, grabbed the golden hued drink and swallowed the rest. Instead of reading the report again, he searched to see who moderated it. The name read Jack Morrow.

"Jack Morrow?" Chet mumbled. "Why do I know that name?" He took a moment to think, but nothing came to him. He looked for the Contact button and clicked it. Scanning the names, he knew two, Alex Redford and Julia Mechanic, old expedition members. He knew Alex better and wondered if he still used the same phone number? He'd contact him in the morning. His mind began to question why the report garnered an A; it shouldn't have, given it didn't reveal any pictures, video or casts. He found nothing to explain the asterisk. But the report... it was almost something like he had experienced, except for one major exception. These people survived their encounter. He gazed at the empty glass he held at his fingertips.

"One more small one."

Chet woke up at the desk, the side of his face firmly planted onto the flat surface. A thin line of drool trailed from his mouth forming into a small pool. Blinking a few times, he focused on the gold tint of liquid still in the glass inches away from his face.

"That explains it," he said to himself as he sat upright while rubbing his eyes. A slight thud pounded in his skull. He looked at the computer and saw it went into sleep mode. He moved the mouse to activate it. The Contact page came up. Chet nodded, remembering he wanted to call Alex if he in fact still used the same telephone number. He hadn't talked to him in eight years. Alex came to visit a couple of times early in his incarceration, but like many others, soon stopped coming. Chet understood. It hurt that people who did visit began to disappear. Dr. Drasner helped him in dealing with those feelings.

Chet rummaged through boxes his sister collected from his old apartment. He hoped to find a few address books. Going through a fifth box, he wrapped his fingers around a leather-bound book, thin. He pulled it out feeling relieved to see at least one of them survived. He flipped through the pages, saw names he'd nearly forgotten. He didn't dwell on those as he flipped over to the R's for Redford. Only one page had names. He ran his fingers along them, scrunched his face with disappointment. It wasn't there. He did a double check. To his great relief, he had passed over Alex's name. Holding his finger just below the number, he picked up the phone on his desk and dialed.

"Hello?" a voice said after two rings.

"Yes," Chet said, his mind stumbling to say something. "I'm looking for Alex Redford."

"Speaking," Alex said, the edge coming off his voice.

"Alex... this is Chet. Chet Daniels."

A moment of silence interceded. "Really?" Alex said not quite certain but also not full of doubt.

"Yes, I'm out. Released a couple weeks ago," Chet said not sure how else to prove his identity.

"Chet!" Alex half shouted with surprise. "I recognize the voice now. Holy Jeez, how are you?"

"I guess as well I can be."

"Wow, it's really you. How can I help? What's going on?"

Chet told him about the report he read on the website and wanted to know more about it. He asked if it was possible for him to contact Jack Morrow. Alex said he would check but didn't think it would be a problem.

"The report out of Willamette State Forest... I'm telling you that hit me," Chet said.

"I imagine it did," Alex said, not sure how to tread into the conversation.

"That isn't all that far from where my life changed," Chet said.

"I know," Alex answered. "A day's hike maybe two at best."

"That sounds right," Chet answered.

Alex hesitated. "I don't know if you know this."

"Know what?"

"Your expedition site. The Controversy... I'm sorry if I don't quite know how to talk about it with you. It's become something of a mythic destination among the Bigfoot community."

"What?" Chet said not sure exactly what he was hearing.

"Your expedition site…it's something of a controversy among people within the community," Alex said. "Do you mind if we discuss this?"

"No, I don't mind," Chet said, surprised by the revelation.

"First of all, people have tried to locate the exact whereabouts of your site. It remains something of an enigma, not exactly sure of its precise location. There are many small clearings up in those elevations. People have claimed to comb every square inch of the region. Some have claimed to find articles of clothing, but nothing has ever materialized as physical proof. And, depending on the group and motive, people are either trying to prove your innocence or your guilt. Like I said, it's become something of a place to make a pilgrimage to. I know of at least a half-dozen attempts to the area. Most have failed because of its remoteness."

"You're kidding?"

"No, not at all. Believe it or not, you're quite the cult figure among some."

"I don't want that," Chet said, his voice going quiet.

"It's not a matter of want ol' friend… It is," Alex said.

"Any sightings in that area?" Chet asked not sure what answer he wanted to hear.

"There's always a report or two but nothing that anyone can really seriously classify above a C grade," Alex said.

"But what about this report I just read?"

"That report is taken very seriously," Sam said.

"Yeah, it garnered a high grade and what's with the asterisk?" Chet asked.

"Well for one… Can I ask for your confidence in this?"

"Absolutely," Chet said sitting up in his chair.

"Have you ever heard of Kyle Marks?"

Chet took a moment to think. "No."

"Look him up on the web, you'll find him. He's an outdoor extremist to some degree. Experienced in big long wilderness hikes, loves the whole bushwhacking thing. He wrote a book about one of his adventures. You'd probably like it," Alex said.

"He filed the report?"

"No. One of the people in the group did. There were four people involved and the initials K. M. appeared with those who had participated in the event. It didn't take a lot to connect the dots given the region and circumstances. I happened to see Kyle a few days ago. He confirmed to me that he was there."

"Bigfoot?"

"He nodded an affirmation to me. He said they saw two, maybe three creatures. Huge, eight to ten feet tall. Walked upright. He never saw anything like it. Not even sure he can rightfully explain it. He wants to keep his name out of it for now. Actually, he requested an amendment to the report to have his initials taken out. I thought it would be done by now. He fears it will hurt his brand."

"That's rich," Chet said with a sarcastic laugh. "Send him my way if he wants to know what a failed brand looks like."

"Are you kidding Chet?" Alex said with disbelief. "You should write a book. Your stock is high. In fact, every fifth e-mail to the site seems to be about you, especially since news of your recent release began to circulate. When exactly did you get out? Everyone within our little world wants to talk to you. I know a couple scientists who would like to speak to you about that trip."

"Well... I don't know about that right now," Chet said with a meek tone. "I don't know if I'm ready for that yet. I just want to get my feet back under me."

"I understand," Alex said. "Hey, how about we get together for dinner. I'll see if Jack's available."

Chet nodded to himself. It actually sounded good. "Yeah, let's do that."

Chapter 7

Jack slowly peeled the bedcovers off his body. He glanced over at his clock, 3:48 am. He turned, smiled. Amy laid peacefully asleep, the covers only hiding her waist and legs. Though they had a 'friends with benefits' relationship, he did truly enjoy making love to her in a deeper, more sensual way. Jack always felt she expressed herself honestly with him emotionally and physically. He liked to think they clicked. Though he knew Amy liked to move about freely in the world, of late, she seemed to enjoy orbiting his world.

Tiptoeing, he went into his office. He took out several maps, both trail and topographic. Spreading them out across the floor, he felt passionate that what he had in mind could be the biggest and most important Bigfoot expedition to occur in the northwest if not the United States. He outlined a plan that involved three parties. Each party would consist of no less than three people, preferably five, spread out in a triangular shape, at no more than a half mile apart. He knew anything more than that and radio contact would start to become sketchy because of the thick terrain. He circled on one of the maps three points he and Pacer believed as the true locations of Chet's expedition sites. He then marked which particular site he believed the Bigfoot attack happened.

Jack looked at the calendar on the wall. He wanted a late August, early September outing. Those months worked best at avoiding rain, but he knew in Oregon, such predictions often came up futile.

Tapping a pencil on one of the maps, he felt two soft hands slide over his shoulders and down his chest.

"Whatcha workin' on?" Amy asked with a warm sultry whisper into his ear. She leaned in and pressed her bare chest against his back. "Busy boy. So dedicated. You know what?"

Jack didn't answer. He just smiled feeling her well-trimmed fingernails scratch his chest.

Amy continued. "You turn me on." She blew lightly into his ear.

Jack turned to face her. He placed his hands on her thighs, ran his fingertips up her smooth skin then swung her into his lap. They smiled at each other before embracing into a long and deep kiss.

Amy pulled away and stood up. "Work. I just wanted to let you know I'm still here." She then peeked in towards Jack's lap. "Nice to see you like what I have to offer."

"Yeah, and thanks for that," he said with an audible exhale watching her walk away, just the dim light from his desk lamp outlining her hour glass figure. He took a moment and wondered if he should follow her. He then remembered that she didn't like needy. She liked focused, strong guys. He turned back to his maps, took a deep breath, pulled a legal pad closer and began to write.

Jack could barely catch his breath when the phone next to his bed rang. He accomplished a lot just a few hours prior but was now dead tired. He stared at the phone. He didn't want to answer, but he found himself reaching for it anyway.

"Hello," he said trying to shake free the mental cobwebs.

"Did I wake you?" the voice asked.

"Yes."

"This is Alex Redford over at…"

"Yeah, hey Alex, what's going on?" Jack asked. Alex didn't call out of the blue for no reason. In fact, he never remembered Alex ever calling his house phone.

"I received a really interesting phone call yesterday," Alex said. "It involves one of your screenings on a report."

Jack swung his legs off the bed so he sat up on its edge. "What? Something wrong?"

Alex laughed. "No, just the opposite really. Chet Daniels read a report you vetted. It sounded eerily like his experience."

"You bet it did," Jack said standing up, still naked.

"Yeah, and guess what, I'm getting together with him for dinner. I thought you might want to join us and fill him in on the details of what you know about the report."

Jack's head swam with excitement. "Absolutely. When?"

"Day after tomorrow, Friday. Dan's Ol-Town Tavern," Alex said. "You know it?"

"Yeah. I've tossed back a few beers there."

"It's not too far out of your way?"

"No friggin' way. This is a chance of a lifetime," Jack said barely holding back his excitement. He noticed his exuberance and dialed it back. "Anything off limits to talk about?"

"We never discussed anything like that, but I'd let the evening's conversation dictate what subject matters are appropriate to touch upon," Alex said. "six o'clock good?"

"Perfect."

"See you then."

Jack held the phone loose in his hand still stunned by his good fortune. It took the dial tone to snap him out of his daze.

"Everything okay?" Amy asked, running a nail lightly down the center of his spine.

Jack turned, smiled while shaking his head. "You're never gonna believe who I'm going to meet."

"I heard Chet's name mentioned," Amy said containing her own excitement. "Is it Chet?"

Jack nodded. "You bet it is."

Amy sprung up on the bed, knees weighing into the mattress and hugged him. "That's so great."

"It is. But not as great as what's coming next," Jack said as he grabbed Amy by the back of her thighs, lifted them with a quick thrust, throwing her onto her back. "I have a special kind of massage in mind for you that I think you're going to love."

Amy grinned, easing her legs further apart. "Do your best. I always love a good tongue massage."

Chapter 8

Corrine sipped on her coffee while staring at the television, not paying attention to the talking head reading the news. She didn't feel right, flushed and clammy. Her eyelids felt like gnomes had tied little anvils to them during a nighttime visit. Picking up her cell phone, she called in sick to work. Before her experience in the woods with Kyle, she had only called in to work once in the last year. Since the incident, four times in a month. Looking out at the beautiful day, the daydream of a peaceful bike ride floated through her imagination. The daydream quickly turned dark. Menacing shadows began to lurk in a thicket of trees, just foggy enough to not make out any details, then, in a snap, a giant ape-like beast appeared in front of her, fully formed, blood dripping from its mouth. Corrine jolted back to reality, her body shuddering, spilling coffee on the table and her lap.

"What's wrong with me?" she mumbled.

Since the occurrence on the camping trip, Corrine hadn't felt right. Nightmares interrupted her sleep more than she wanted to admit. Her concentration on projects at work dwindled. She could not stop the constant nightmarish thoughts that filled her mind because of that night on the mountain... she was thankful they got out alive but for some reason, the incident still haunted her. She didn't blame Kyle for what happened. In fact, she felt safe around him, especially those first couple of days where she decided to sleep at his place.

After witnessing a few of her panic attacks, Kyle suggested she should seek help. She didn't, saying it would pass, but they did not. Six weeks later he began to not return calls or texts. She knew he wanted out. On the few occasions they did communicate, he either had to cancel their getting together or simply didn't have the time to listen to her issues.

Picking up her tablet, she searched for psychiatrists. She highlighted some numbers, even picked up her phone to call but never completed the dialing. "What am I going to say... *I can't get over the Bigfoot experience I had?* They'll have me sign a form, and I'll disappear into some loony bin." Still, she desperately needed to talk to someone about the incident that she could trust.

Changing directions, she Googled the subjects Bigfoot and Willamette State Forest. The first entry that caught her eye gave her a link to a Bigfoot site, *The Bigfoot Research Society*. She clicked it. Skimming through the site, she looked at some pictures, read a few headlines, one about some guy getting out of jail, but didn't pay any attention to it. Then she noticed the 'Reports' section. She clicked and entered. Combing through the information, she marveled at all the sightings, near sightings, and vocalizations. She wasn't unaware of the Bigfoot phenomenon but the subject matter never meant much to her. Yet now, she sat mesmerized by it all.

"Oh my God," she said nearly dropping her coffee cup. Staring at the screen, she couldn't believe she was reading about her incident on the website. Her hands began to shake. "What the hell," she muttered. Upset, frightened, pissed, she clicked over to find the site administrators, found Alex and Julia's name. She wanted phone numbers, but none appeared. She thought about Kyle. He didn't do this. It isn't like him. *No, he would have made it more grandiose, self-serving.* She wondered if he even knew about this report. *It was one of the others.* She looked again at the report. The name at the end said Rob H. *That bastard. Why?* Corrine glanced at her shaking hand. She clenched it into a fist so it would stop. Her mind raced with thoughts of thousands if not millions of people reading about her harrowing experience in the woods. She felt violated as if all these unknown readers would all of a sudden see her pain, her anxiety, her weakness. She flipped the tablet, pushed it away, balled up in her chair and began to cry.

Chapter 9

Alex sat at the bar of Dan's Ol Towne Tavern. The establishment's décor saluted the art of dark wood. The bar, the walls, the trim, the floor, all had some shade of light sucking dark to it that made one feel as if they had entered a cave. Built in the late 19th century by Dan Hogle, it became the town's local watering hole and managed to always have someone from the family line run it.

Despite various offerings by investors to take it over and remodel it into a personality numbing, processed food filled franchise; the family worked at keeping the place looking as authentic to its origins as possible, uneven, creaky wooden floors and all. Alex knew the history but wished for a few more light fixtures. Soft tungsten bulbs lit the entire place and barely. The positioning of lamps and other light sources appeared designed by engineers looking to create the least user-friendly lighting scenarios possible. With small windows unevenly laid out, most facing north, even a daytime visit on a clear blue-sky day didn't offer much relief in terms of light.

With a tall glass of beer in one hand, Alex checked e-mails and played a trivia game on his phone while he waited for his guests. Every few seconds he'd scan the place, glance at his watch, take a sip, and repeat.

"Hey old friend," a cheerful voice said.

Alex whipped his head up, wide smile at the ready before it faded into a grin.

"Nice to see you too," Jack said, a touch insulted at the reaction. "Sorry, I'm not the rock star."

Alex laughed. "My apologies. Glad you could make it."

"Thanks," Jack said as he sat on the stool next to him. "But it's going to cost you a beer to mend my hurt feelings."

"Of course it will," Alex said waving for the bartender to bring over another beer.

Jack hadn't taken more than a couple sips when he spotted Chet standing in the foyer, instantly recognizing him from the years of pictures he looked at that were seared into his brain. He tapped Alex, alerting him. "Aside from looking like some of the life has been sucked out of him, he hasn't changed much."

Alex turned, stood up and waved for Chet to join them. Chet nodded and walked towards the two men.

"My goodness, you're looking well," Alex said. He lied. He could see prison had worn out some of the exuberance that Chet used to carry. The man Alex knew stood taller, had a strong chin, shoulders held firm, robust hair. The Chet that stood before him now appeared worn out, stressed, shoulders more slumped, thin, touches of gray streaks streaming through his hair. It was the same man, but certainly not the same person.

"I'm still trying to get my feet back on the ground," Chet said with a shy grin. "Everything moves so fast sometimes. Just trying to catch up on all the news and technology, I can't believe how much things have changed. Still… I'm getting there."

"Can I get you a beer? Can you have a beer?" Alex asked.

"I don't remember my probation officer saying I couldn't. I have to take an occasional drug test, but she didn't forbid alcohol."

"So a beer it is," Alex said as he waved for another one. "Chet, I want to introduce a friend. He's a real up and comer. More than that now really," he turned Chet towards Jack's direction. "This is Jack Morrow. He's a trusted friend, co-worker and a leader now on the research end. He's put together some impressive expeditions. He's also the guy who vetted that report you read on the site."

The two shook hands and exchanged pleasantries. Alex didn't see any suspicion from Chet and hoped Chet didn't mind the extra company.

"So… let's grab a table and have something to eat," Alex said.

The appetizers came - quick, mozzarella sticks, calamari, and stuffed mushrooms in all their salty, cheesy deliciousness. The beer flowed easily, and the three men relaxed into general banter as they checked out the bevy of women who came and went. Chet shared some prison stories knowing that would be the great curiosity aside from what put him there in the first place. Alex and Jack acknowledged the subject, but both worked to not dwell on it. They could both see the physical toll it took on Chet and rather than focus on the past, opted to steer things towards a more positive future.

After the fifth round of the local IPA beer made it into their hands and they toasted each other, Chet broke the ice. "I know you guys want to hear my story. What I saw. Am I interested in an expedition and all that?" He looked down at his rough fingernails, noticing how he continued to pick at them. "I just want you to know that I haven't decided on what I want to do regarding searching for Bigfoot. I've struggled with it. I'd like to forget, start a whole new life and move on, but my mind always comes back to it. I fear it may always be with me. But know this…" and he stared into each of their eyes. "I did not kill those people. You can believe what you want and if there is one thing I've come to peace with, is that there will be others who aren't going to believe me. I know there is very little I can do about it." Chet leaned back in his chair and blew out a large exhale straight up into the air above him. He felt like a new man.

"I'm so glad I could express that. You have no idea the

weight that carries."

Alex reached over and squeezed his shoulder. He had a little bit of a beer buzz going. "Glad to have you back," he said with a broad smile.

Jack had remained mostly quiet, preferring to listen, adding a comment here and there. He saw the moment as an entry point to offer more to the conversation. "Well, I for one never thought you did it if that's any consolation."

Chet nodded. "Thank you."

"Yeah, in fact, I've visited the site where the events took place."

A weird silence ensued, like an invisible coating of molasses poured over the scene. Both of their eyes turned to Chet. He didn't appear angry. He didn't reveal any emotion. Chet looked as if he needed to process the statement. Alex mentioned to Chet that the site had become something of a pilgrimage for Squatchers, but hearing it in person seemed to put Chet into a moment of pause.

"What did you think of it?" Chet asked, not sure what else to say.

"My honest opinion?" Jack said.

"Please," Chet said sitting up, wrapping both hands around his glass of beer. "I have to get used to what others have to say. I'm game."

"I think the authorities searched in the wrong area," Jack said with a frank, matter-of-fact tone.

Chet sat silent. His face tightened right in front of them. He blinked a couple times slowly. Chet took hold of his beer and raised it to his mouth. Closing his eyes, he took a bigger than normal sip before putting the mug down on the table with a gentle touch. "And how pre'-tell can you make that assumption."

Jack wondered if he revealed news about his found video footage if it would be like an assault on the senses and overwhelm him. "I went over various maps that I could find showing the area the cops and forest service investigated. Then myself and a friend, Pacer Bradford, went into the region and spent some time exploring those sites."

Chet listened. He didn't move at all, holding steady like a wax figurine of himself.

Jack continued. "And, based on notes I acquired from Paul Jorgenson's ex-girlfriend, I thought the description of the sites he wrote about from scouting the area differed than some of the sites the investigators explored."

Chet still said nothing.

Jack took this gesture as a cue to continue. "I'll explain the details of how I acquired the notes later, but suffice it to say, Pacer and I hiked up into that region, explored those sites noted by the police, then moved west, just out of the zone where the cops searched. We found locations that better resembled what Paul wrote about and what the video showed."

"Whoa," Chet said, stopping the conversation dead cold. He sat up straight, pulled himself closer to the table then began to lean in towards Jack. "Video? What video?"

Jack hadn't meant to let that slip the way it did, but he didn't regret it. The fact about a video was now out there. "In an area just outside the search zone where we found several other clearings. It was there I discovered a camera."

"I'm sorry," Chet said, his voice sounding totally stunned. "You found a camera? Paul Jorgenson's camera?"

Jack took a deep breath. He glanced over at Alex who was also hearing about this news for the first time. Jack could see the look of wide-eyed surprise cross his face. "A couple weeks before your release, I found the video camera Paul used to tape your expedition in one of the clearings up there. It was lodged deep into a rotting tree."

Chet sat stone-faced, no blinking, frozen as if someone stopped time.

"You okay?" Alex asked after a few silent seconds.

Chet's eyes shifted towards Alex without his head moving an inch. They then closed for a good ten seconds before opening again. "You are saying that there is video evidence of the expedition?"

Jack nodded. "More than that... of the attack."

Chet pulled his lips into his mouth as he bowed his head towards the beer in front of him. Feelings of anger, relief, sadness, collided like comets into his brain. His legs went numb for a moment. He wanted to speak, but words would not coalesce in his mouth.

Alex asked again if he was okay.

Chet felt like he was catapulted out into some timeless void. He heard Alex ask him if he was all right but the voice sounded far away and hollow. It took a moment to snap back into the present. Finally, Chet blinked his eyes a few times. "I'm fine. Stunned."

"You look a little flushed," Alex said.

That quip gave Chet a chuckle. "You think?"

"Sorry," Jack said, looking at both of them. "I just had no way to easily introduce the subject."

Chet nodded. "Yeah... there really isn't any easy way to drop that in, is there?"

"Just so you know, there isn't much footage that survived," Jack added. "Exactly seven minutes and forty-five seconds. Much of it is grainy, pixelated, or just flat out dark."

"How much of the attack? I mean... do you see them?" Chet asked composed and serious before taking another slow sip of beer.

Jack waited a moment. "You do. Not well but you see them."

"I need to see it at some point," Chet said with a more somber tone, straightening his body in the chair. "I can already feel a certain anxiety overcoming me, but I need to see it, to face it... to know the last twelve years of my life haven't all gone for naught."

"I have it with me," Jack said.

Chet bobbed his head as if someone had replaced his neck with a spring. "How? Here? Now?"

Jack nodded. "On my tablet."

"You can do that?" Chet asked, his mind still in a swirl of stunned amazement.

"Now you can," Alex chimed in.

Chet raised his eyebrows. "Wow. Okay, let's see it."

Jack pulled his tablet out, hit the power and waited for it to boot up. "Good thing I have 4G/LTE otherwise, we'd have to rely on the Wi-Fi here and who knows how well it would run in this place."

"It's on a cloud?" Alex asked.

"Yeah," Jack said, staring at the screen. "I didn't want to take the chance of storing it on the hard drive, and then have some freak thing happen, like I lose it, or someone steals it."

Chet looked at both of them as if they spoke a foreign language. "I wish I knew what you were talking about, but I'll take your word for it."

Alex grinned. "Don't worry. You'll catch up soon enough."

Chet turned back to Jack watching him tap away at the device. Chet had seen tablets. Various prison officials used them. Even Dr. Drasner, his psychiatrist, used them every so often, but Chet never asked about the purposes of the devices.

"Ready?" Jack said holding the tablet out for Chet to take. "Just hit the arrow and it will play."

Chet took the device, holding it like a fragile piece of art. He leaned it against the top edge of the table and held his finger above the tablet for a suspended moment, grimaced, then pressed the arrow.

Starting with footage at the base camp, Chet felt himself catapulted back in time. He'd pictured the member's faces a million times, but now, watching the screen, they all somehow appeared different, younger, not quite how his mind had painted them.

"Can I stop it? I just want to see their faces," Chet asked holding the device up, straining to keep his emotions in check.

"Of course," Jack said, sliding up next to him. "Just tap the bottom of the screen there and you'll see the timeline come up. You see those two slashes that look like the Roman Numerals for two, just tap that and the footage will pause. If you want to go back, place your finger on the timeline and slide it back, then hit the arrow."

Chet thought the instructions easy enough but fumbled the execution.

"Where do you want to go to?" Jack said taking a firmer hold on the device.

"The beginning."

Chet watched the video several times. At first, he just wanted to see the faces of the people he once called friends. He'd worked with many of them several times, hiked and camped with Hollis, and Brandon, slept with Melanie twice, drunken hookups. He touched the screen as if wanting to touch their skin. He could feel tears well up, but he fought them off.

When he came to the attack, his whole body deadened. He couldn't even feel himself holding the tablet. As the footage unfolded he thought he might break out into a panic attack, but to his own surprise, he watched it, cold, without much feeling, just objectivity as if studying facts. All his emotions of the event left him. Then the screen went black.

Chet handed the tablet back. "I've seen enough."

"Well?" Jack said. "What did you think? You sat there silent the entire time."

Chet didn't know what to think. The beasts on the video were dark, barely definable but he filled in the blanks just fine with his own recollection and imagination. "Thank you," he said. He couldn't think of anything more to say.

"Too much to process?" Alex asked.

"I don't know… maybe," Chet answered. "I thought I would feel more… but it's like dead to me. I thought it would confirm what I had to say all along. It does, don't get me wrong, but inside, it just..." Chet stopped, not able to express himself, thoughts shooting through his mind too quick to get a handle on. "Maybe, because in some way, I buried it all a long time ago. I was more moved by seeing them all at the campsite, alive, smiling."

"It's a lot to take in," Jack said. "I have the footage on a flash drive you can have."

"I don't know what that is but thanks," Chet said, a feeling of exhaustion overcoming him. "When did you say you found this?"

"About two weeks before your release," Jack said.

Chet nodded. "I see. Wouldn't have done much good to show it to anyone. Probably just cause more trouble than it's worth." Chet could feel the words come out of his mouth without emotion, like a zombie of sorts. He touched his fresh glass of beer that had just come. The cold of the mug helped settle his thinking. "I have to say… thank you for not making this public. It would only bring the kind of attention that I really don't want." Chet said feeling more relaxed. "I've had my fill of cameras and controversy. Personally, I'm just hoping to slip back into anonymity, write and review stuff under a pseudonym and move on."

Jack and Alex gazed at Chet with disbelief.

"You're kidding, right?" Jack blurted.

Alex whacked Jack's arm with the back of his hand. "It's his business, not yours."

Chet waved Alex off. "It's okay. I get it. I've read a number of forums and articles on how my experience both helped and hurt Bigfoot research. I know there are people out there who want me to get in front of a camera and bring attention to the subject."

Jack saw an opportunity to address his ambitious goal. "Now that you have put it out there, I would love for you to join me on an expedition back to where the attack happened. Like I said, the authorities, I believe, searched the wrong area. The video proves that. I think we can put an end to the Bigfoot debate once and for all."

"It's some remarkable footage, but I'm sure the cops and investigators can, and will come up with a good explanation for that footage," Chet said.

Jack nodded. "Maybe. Let me ask, do you remember how many investigators combed that entire area? Fifty, Seventy-five?"

"I guess," Chet responded. "If I recall my lawyer right, I think that's about how many went through that region of the forest. They found nothing... not a blood stain on a rock, any equipment, clothing, the place was bare."

"I know. That's what they kept saying," Jack said with a disbelieving smug look. "However, Pacer and I, just the two of us, spent three days up there and not only did we find the video and camera, but we found these as well." Jack pulled out two distinctly different buttons and placed them on the table.

Chet's face went white. He instinctively reached out and grabbed the smaller one, a little faux silver button with an eagle design on it and metal loop on the back. He held it up to his face. He could feel tears well up as he turned the small button around in his fingers.

"You recognize it?" Jack asked sounding more like a statement.

"Yes," Chet mumbled. He placed the button down and leaned away from the table. "It was Melanie's."

"Are you sure?" Alex asked.

Chet chortled. "The first time we slept together. I unbuttoned those buttons because I made a comment about them. I made some shitty remark about how another eagle is going to land or something cheesy like that."

Jack felt he had momentum and didn't want to let it go. "What about this other button. Do you recognize it?"

Again, Chet nodded studying the solid brown hard plastic button with a metallic rim. "Looks like it came off Hollis's field jacket."

"You sure?" Jack asked.

"You found these close together?" Chet asked.

"Relatively, about thirty feet apart," Jack said.

"Well, if you've been up there, you know it's not one of those well-trodden regions. No one is simply passing through, let alone losing two buttons that close together," Chet said. He shook his head. Thoughts of the investigation, the interrogations, flashed through his mind. He bit at the anger he could feel swirling deep within him. He promised himself he would put that all away. Anger had consumed him enough those first several years behind bars. Dr. Drasner helped him move past it, and taught him how to become 'more present.' Drasner drilled it home how holding on to the past could eat away at a person's soul. It took time, but he learned to forgive. He was never quite certain exactly what he was forgiving, but he understood Dr. Drasner's basic premise. It worked. But now, the anger built. *All those years...*

"All this evidence could help clear your name," Jack offered.

Chet stamped down the fury but not enough to shoot back an answer quickly and pointedly. "Nothing will ever totally clear my name. I accept that. You can't paint over people's minds. They'll judge on their own perceptions. There's nothing I can do but move on."

Jack backed off. He could see Chet's emotion building up. He presented Chet with a lot of information, maybe too much. "Sorry."

Chet put up his hand. "It's okay. You've given me a lot to process. It's good. Take it head on." He picked up what he believed was Melanie's button again, examined it, ran his fingers along its ridges. "The way things went in that trial; I think these may have caused me more harm than good. They screwed me over with the flimsiest of circumstantial evidence. This may have sealed their case to put me away forever."

They all sat silent for a moment, just the noise of the bar and the growing crowd filling the void.

Jack's ambition churned within. He knew letting the moment stew would work against him. "Then how about that trip back? I have a group who is willing to go," Jack said.

"That's a lot to handle right now," Chet said. "Believe me, it's intriguing. Don't think I haven't thought about it."

"I know someone else who would love to be involved," Alex said. He watched, as the two other men seemed to know whom he would say. "Sam Ashford. He's got the latest and best equipment."

"Yeah, but the man just said he's trying not to bring attention to himself," Jack said in defense of Chet. "Sam brings a lot of spotlight with his presence."

"Thanks," Chet said. "It's okay. I understand the suggestions. But right now… I have to think about this whole thing. I'm sorry, but I can't just give you an answer at this moment."

"Absolutely. I understand," Jack said as he leaned back into his chair and clapped his hands. "How about we order some more food? Take our minds off all this information."

"That sounds like a great idea," Alex added.

"Not a bad looking crowd either," Jack noted as he looked around the bar. "I'll bet this whole scene with lots of women walking around is a nice change of pace."

Chet laughed as he too looked about the tavern. There were a lot more people now than when he first entered. "Much nicer."

"Bet it would be great to meet a woman," Alex said.

Chet just grinned. "A woman. That would be nice."

Chapter 10

Corrine woke up in a heap of sweat. She panted heavy, her chest heaving as she took in huge gulps of air. Her head spun in confusion. Feeling lightheaded, she clutched the sheets with her fists to gain balance as she sat up. Tears streamed down her face, mixing with the perspiration that soaked her skin. It happened again, a middle of the night panic attack. Closing her eyes, she feared looking over at the clock.

"Please don't be 2:23," she mumbled aloud. Opening her eyes into a squint, she glimpsed over at the cable box on her nightstand, it read 2:23, then changed to 2:24. "Damn it."

Corrine let herself fall back onto her mattress, her head flopping into the top of two pillows. Staring at the ceiling, she tried to think of how many 'middle of the night anxiety attacks' had happened since her trip with Kyle. "Too many," she answered herself. She felt like her attacks were now happening more frequently.

"This has to stop," she said, having calmed down, but now pissed off at herself. She got up. After a brief initial stretch, she went into her bathroom and poured herself a cup of water. Staring into the mirror, she could see the dark circles that had begun to form. She stared at herself muttering she had to get it together. Touching the skin just under her eyes, she knew there was only so much makeup she could use to mask the darkening area.

She tossed the cup in the garbage and looked at herself again. "Get it together girl." Walking back to bed, she thought of Kyle. Kyle didn't suffer any anxiety from the event. In fact, he told her he was thinking about writing a detailed account about the incident, contemplating a novella should the right opportunity present itself. He said she should write about her feelings as a way of possibly exorcising the demons haunting her.

"Come on Corrine," she said looking at herself in the dresser mirror. "You have to get up in three hours for work."

Corrine sat at her work cubicle bouncing a pencil eraser against the edge of her desk. The rhythm had no sense to it. She blissfully pounded away, unaware of her poor drumming.

"Hey girl," her friend and co-worker Betty Grafton said with her usual zest; hips and legs in a constant shifting mode as if pivoting on a fashion runway.

It snapped Corrine out of her daydream, startling her to the point of losing a grip on the pencil, it falling to the floor then rolling underneath her desk.

"You didn't need that anyway," Betty said with a bright red lipstick smile to match her bright orange, yellow and red one-piece dress that revealed her well-toned curves and calves.

"I'm sorry. A little distracted I guess," Corrine said not looking at her.

"Yeah... for about three weeks," Betty replied, her smile fading. "It's become noticeable."

The color drained from Corrine's face.

"And for these soulless robots to notice, you know you're off your game," Betty said. She then flashed a smile and performed a quick body bob, dipping at the knees to get closer to Corrine. "Not to worry, I've tried to cover for you." She then bounced back a step. "On the upside, what do you think of my new outfit?" Betty gave a quick twirl to show off all sides.

"I'm so sorry," Corrine said putting her hands to her face, her eyes shimmering with tears.

"Stop right there," Betty said while kicking out her hip into a defiant pose, an over the top gesture she used for dramatic flair to accentuate a point. "After work, we're going out for drinks. You need to get off your chest whatever's been bothering you. Betty Bop here is just the girl you need to set you on a straight path," she said pointing at herself. "You do the spilling and I'll do the listening. When you're finished, we'll figure a way to clean up all this emotional untidiness."

Corrine cracked a reserved smile. "I appreciate it... your concern, but what's on my mind isn't anything you can help me with."

Betty raised one of her meticulously trimmed and liner heightened dark eyebrows. "I've heard all the stories, and no matter how bizarre, they all have a simple solution to them. Your problem is you just can't see the forest through the trees right now."

Corrine laughed. "You have no idea how close to the truth you are."

"Great then," Betty said, showing her big smile, and overly white teeth gleaming with delight. She looked at her watch. "An hour to go. Try to pretend like you're getting something done and I'll swing by when it's time to leave." Betty took two steps before stopping and turning around. "Hey, I asked how you liked my outfit, and you didn't answer."

Corrine gave her a look over. Betty never disappointed when it came to loud clothes. "Very Katy Perry, *This is How We Do.*"

Betty smiled wide. "That's what I was going for." She then curtsied. "Thank you."

The Happy Hour crowd packed the bar. Betty knew a bartender and managed to get her and Corrine a table in the back corner, away from the flirting and cheap pick-up lines, so they could have some peace. The outgoing and confident Betty felt derision for folks who desperately paraded their flesh for attention. Though she dressed stylishly and sometimes loud, she always kept a modest approach to how much skin she would show.

"Here you are ladies," the young, good-looking, broad-shouldered bartender said as he gave Betty a friendly wink before seating them. "Can I get you drinks?"

"Thanks, Paul," Betty said returning his wink with a playful smile. "We'll have two Cosmopolitans."

Corrine shook her head. "I don't drink Cosmopolitans."

"Have you ever had one?" Betty asked.

"No, I don't think so," Corrine answered.

Betty turned to Paul. "Two Cosmo's please and how's your mom doing?"

"She's doing better," Paul said with a grateful grin. "I'll tell her you asked about her, and I'll have those drinks over to you in a minute."

Betty turned back to Corrine. "You seem more comfortable."

Corrine leaned back against the dark wood headboard that separated the booths from each other. "I'm tired."

"I can tell," Betty said. "You haven't been your usual friendly or energetic self of late. People have talked, wondering what's up. You and that guy break up?"

Corrine glanced towards the ceiling before turning her eyes to Betty. "That's run its course, but it isn't the reason for my funk."

Betty shot her a *then what* expression, raising her eyebrows while pursing her pouty red lips.

Corrine felt uncomfortable about how to express herself. She hadn't discussed the incident with anyone. Kyle didn't want to hear any more about her problems. The other woman, Teresa, didn't want to connect and her boyfriend, Rob, wore the occurrence like a badge of honor. Corrine wanted to tell some old friends, but since she had moved away from San Francisco five year's prior, those ties had waned.

She had newer friends, but she feared that this kind of disclosure would have them running for the hills.

Corrine leaned forward. "Okay, but you have to make a promise."

Betty nodded and told her she was in.

"You remember that camping trip I did six weeks ago?" Corrine asked.

"I remember you telling me about going on it... with that guy who wrote the book. The one you met at the convention," Betty said, the recall coming into focus.

"Yeah, Kyle. Well, something happened that was so strange, bizarre, terrifying... I haven't been able to shake it."

"Oh God, this isn't some bizarre sex ritual thing, is it?" Betty said contorting her face.

Corrine half-smiled. "In retrospect, I wish."

"Really? Try to get kinky, and it got out of hand?" Betty said with intrigue in her voice.

Before Corrine could continue, the drinks arrived.

Betty raised her glass. "To the unknown."

Corrine wondered why Betty chose that expression. It seemed strangely appropriate. She took an extra big swallow of the drink and let the sting of the liquor pour through her.

"So, back to the bizarre," Betty said holding the glass in both hands, bright orange fingernails flailing, anticipating the story.

"Anyway, we were camping in some spot in the middle of nowhere out in Willamette State Park. I don't like leaving the trail for the absolute unknown, but Kyle and his friends got off on that stuff. He assured me we'd stay on a conservative course. It was for the most part. Well, one night, late, I turned in before everyone else. They stayed up keeping the fire going, chatting about nothing in particular, when all of a sudden the forest went dead quiet."

"That would creep me out," Betty said. "But I'm not a woods person as you know."

"It did creep me out," Corrine said. "Anyway, Kyle has me come out of the tent and all four of us are standing wondering what the hell was happening. I thought maybe a bear was around or a mountain lion."

"The woods wouldn't go quiet for that, would it?" Betty asked.

"No, not at all," Corrine said. "But that's exactly what was going on – dead silence, like some scene from a horror movie."

"That's freaky. I'd be scared shitless."

"Believe me, I'd take the silence over what happened next," Corrine said as she recounted how at least two, maybe three or more tall, dark, hairy creatures surrounded the camp and assaulted them with rocks. She related how helpless and frozen in place they all were as these shadowy beasts seemed to circle them, studying, picking a strategy of unknown intent. Then just as they thought the episode was over, one of the creatures appeared within the circle of light the fire gave off, revealing its horrifying presence and howling in their faces. Then as fast as it appeared, the creature vanished back into the shadows of the woods.

Corrine let out a long exhale, picked up her drink and again took a larger than normal gulp.

Betty sat back. She bit her lower lip. Her normally bright eyes glazed over, bewildered.

"I'd take the whacky sex," Corrine said seeing Betty's confused expression.

"You think?" Betty answered.

"This is what haunts me almost every night," Corrine said. "I'm having a hard time shaking it. I can't sleep."

Betty sat back up. "It's a bizarre story."

"You can understand my reticence at sharing it."

"I can. Have any of them talked about it?"

Tears filled Corrine's eyes. "Kyle didn't want to hear about it after the first couple weeks of nightmares, anxiety attacks, insomnia, whatever it all is I'm going through. He thinks I just need to get over it."

Betty rolled her big blue eyes. "Such a dick."

"It isn't like we had invested a lot of time into each other," Corrine said. "And I pulled away too. I didn't help the situation. He did suggest I see someone about this."

"You don't have to defend him," Betty said. "Even if he didn't want to pursue the relationship, he doesn't have to be insensitive to your feelings."

It was Corrine's turn to roll her eyes. "We're not talking about any guy here. This is an ego guy, a guy who'll likely love that this happened to him. I'm sure there's another book in this somehow. He's even told me he's thinking about it."

"I don't care," Betty said. "This is the 21st century, not caveman days. Even if he wants to be a man's man, he should at least have the sense if not the decency to treat your troubles with respect."

"I'm not saying he shouldn't, but I really wasn't expecting too much," Corrine said. "I mean, I acted coldly to it at times. It wasn't like he totally froze me out. I have to take some of the blame."

Betty pushed her tongue into her cheek. "Then listen to me and listen good. You are getting exactly what you put into this. If you wanted to build up this psychological wall, you did exactly that." She took a sip of her drink. "And if I can be frank about this, you have to own this situation. Regardless of this Kyle guy, whether he was a dick or not, it's up to you to put this behind you."

Corrine felt a rush of rejection. Tears began to well up, but she didn't outright cry. In fact, she felt better once the initial jolt of adrenaline passed. She knew she had to take control of her circumstances. No one else could help her do that. She stared at Betty. "Thank you. Thank you for that wake-up call."

Betty smiled wide and bobbed her head, the full length of

her thick long dark curly hair following her movement in a wave. "That's what I do. I do truth."

"Yeah, but is it going to stop the nightmares? I feel better getting that off my chest, but I don't think that's the cure all for it."

"It won't hurt. You had all that emotion bottled up. That's never good. At the very least, you should breathe a little better."

"Do you believe me?"

Betty had listened with rapt attention. The story seemed too strange to believe. But she also knew Corrine and knew it wasn't in her to make up a tale as wild, detailed and creative as the one she just heard. "Sweetheart, I don't know anything about Bigfoot, but I'm also not in any position to say what you saw isn't true. You obviously experienced something because I have personally seen how it has affected you. And this Kyle guy doesn't sound like he's worth making up that kind of story for."

It wasn't the exact answer Corrine was looking for, but she took it. She felt a great deal of relief having expressed herself. Now, she just wanted some girl talk, a few laughs and yes, check out some of the random guys who came and went.

When Corrine peeked at her watch, she noticed it was already after nine o'clock. She had to do a double-take. They'd been chatting and laughing for over three hours. She couldn't remember how many drinks they ordered, but knew they both needed to take taxis home.

"I can't believe how late it's getting," Corrine said as she lightly swirled her nearly finished drink.

"We should have at least one more then, shouldn't we?" Betty slurred, her once strong smile, now a sloppy one.

It sounded good to Corrine who held her liquor and composure with more grace. "Okay, but first I have to use the ladies room."

"I'll order," Betty said with a salute.

Corrine carefully slid out of the booth and stood up. She took a breath, relieved her legs didn't give out under her. Placing a hand on the table, she shook herself, snapping some sense back together. Raising an eyebrow towards Betty, she announced she was ready to go.

The bar/restaurant remained packed as a slightly different crowd of people filtered in. Earlier it had been wall to wall after-work professionals of all ages, now the crowd gravitated towards a nightlife scene, younger, twenties – compared to their mid-thirties age. The attire also turned far more casual as tighter tops, and jeans began to take center stage. Corrine wasn't a bar scene person, having shed that lifestyle when she left San Francisco. She went out from time to time, but this setting wasn't her speed.

After zigzagging her way through some people, she felt her phone vibrate just as she came to a gap in the crowd. She took it out of her back pocket to see who texted her. She wasn't looking up when she smacked face first into a man's chest.

"I'm sorry," Corrine said, embarrassed.

"My fault totally," the man replied. "I wasn't watching where I was going. My apologies."

"I wasn't paying attention either," Corrine said as she glanced over the tallish man before her, dark brown hair, strong chin, thin but looked fit. She liked what she saw.

"Distracted by the oddity of the scene?" the man asked as he looked back over towards the crowded section of the bar.

Corrine concurred. "Yes. I'm not really used to this kind of scene."

"Me too. It's been a while," the man said.

Corrine caught the man's riveting blue eyes stare into her equally blue ones. They just stood outside the bathroom doors holding each other in a momentary gaze.

"Sorry," the man half blushed. "I don't know why I did that. I hope I didn't put you off."

Corrine smiled. "Not at all. It was nice."

The man grinned back. "It was… my name is Chet."

"Corrine. Nice to meet you, Chet."

Another moment of silence ensued. "Can I buy you a drink?" Chet asked.

Corrine smiled. "I'm here with a friend. But I don't think she'll mind."

"Then it wouldn't be very gentlemanly of me if I didn't offer to buy her one as well."

Chapter 11

Chet agreed to go over to Jack's place with Alex the next day. After meeting Corrine at the bar, he excused himself from the guys who had no problem with Chet pursuing finer company. Chet appreciated the backslapping, thumbs up and smiles the guys gave him. It felt good to have some comradery.

"You dog," Jack said when he opened the door to his place and saw Chet wear a wide smile.

Chet bashfully nodded. "I won't lie. It felt great talking to a woman who wasn't my sister, my probation officer or some prison personnel."

"I'll bet it did," Jack said as he let Chet and Alex in pointing towards his living room where they could talk.

Chet and Alex took seats on Jack's sofa, which was positioned center up to watch the nice 57-inch television mounted on the wall. Moving beyond pleasantries, Jack asked if anyone needed something to drink. Chet asked for water while Alex said he was fine.

Coming back with a tall glass of water, Jack handed it to Chet before taking a seat. "I'm going to get to the point. Several of them. One thing that is never addressed in any detail is your story on how you escaped the attack?"

Alex looked over to Chet, curious to hear the story.

Chet took a moment. "I ran," he said peering off as if his memory projected the vision onto some distant screen. "I ran as fast as I could. There was screaming. The terror in their screams echoed through the woods, and then, nothing. The woods went quiet... then I ran faster."

"How did you know which way to go?" Jack asked.

"I didn't. I just ran," Chet said. "I kept going down the slope of the mountain until I came to one of the service roads. I don't know how long I was running for, but I knew I could run more." Chet paused to collect his thoughts. "Those things. They came out of the shadows. They were just there in our camp, and they moved with such speed. Once I realized there was nothing I could do against them or for the crew, I ran. I could have sworn I saw others run off," Chet paused, looking into his glass before continuing. "I know this much… when I came to the road, I looked up to see where the sun was. It was sometime in the afternoon. I knew west was the direction I had to go. I ran."

"Did you see them again? Bigfoot?" Alex asked.

Chet shook his head. "I saw nothing again, just trees."

Jack sat up on the edge of his couch cushion. "Did you hear anything? Another call or a scream?"

Chet paused. He pictured himself back out on the secluded, hard packed dirt road. Trees lined every direction he could see. The world around him stood silent and motionless. He remembered looking for tire tracks and not seeing anything that appeared recent. He couldn't remember pausing for more than a couple seconds before breaking out into another run.

"Not that I recall," Chet said slowly bringing himself back to the present moment. "I breathed so hard from running, and my mind raced with all kinds of bizarre thoughts. I just wanted to get as far away as I could. It doesn't sound brave but at the time, I was simply trying to survive."

"How long did it take for you to reach someone?" Alex asked.

Chet shrugged. "It's been so long. I've tried to block so much of it all out." He paused as if to search his mind for more to say. "What do the transcripts say? I'm sure there's an official timeline somewhere."

"And I have something like that," Jack said walking out of his living room and into his office. He pulled open a drawer to his desk and took out some papers. He had visualized this day and made sure all the materials about the case were within fingertips distance. Rifling through the stack of papers, he stopped at a page, ran his fingers down it until he spotted what he was looking for.

"It says you made contact with the driver of a logging truck, Paul Gorsen, at approximately 3 pm. That puts your incident at roughly eight or nine hours old," Jack said. He then glared at Chet with some astonishment. "You ran for nine hours?"

"I don't know exactly how much I ran, but it was most of it. And if it weren't for that driver, I would have kept running."

"You never stopped for any breaks?" Alex asked.

"Maybe. I can't really remember," Chet said. "Short ones."

"I don't think I can run five miles let alone all that distance and downhill to boot," Jack said staring at the paperwork before glancing at his own ever-growing waistline.

"You could. Believe me," Chet said.

"You know, this probably explains why you might not have related the proper location of your camp to the police," Alex added. "You were so out of it; possibly even in some form of legitimate shock that you couldn't think straight, despite believing so."

Chet nodded. "I know. The shrinks all said similar things. My defense said I wasn't mentally stable enough to lead investigators to the proper site. The prosecution countered saying my knowledge of the region was better than most and I was quite capable of locating the proper spot. A bunch of legal shit took place that played out for the prosecution."

"Sometimes it seems that it really comes down to who can out lawyer who, rather than being about seeking justice," Alex added.

"As far as I'm concerned, they checked the wrong areas," Jack interjected.

Jack took out the same topographic map he had shown his expedition group and unfolded it. He pointed to the region

Chet led authorities. "The biggest problem is that they should have investigated an area five hundred yards west of where they stopped," he said tapping his finger on a point on the map where he and Pacer camped.

"And you're saying the cops never investigated the site you found this video?" Chet asked.

Jack nodded. "According to transcripts I could access, conversations with people who either searched the woods or had talked with people who participated in the search, it seems by my estimation, they missed it. Maya Hanson, a supporter of yours and Bigfoot enthusiast, Alex knows her, she knew one of the cops who spent a lot of time working the woods, and she said her friend pointed out all the locations they investigated on a map. Jacob Hollins, another friend who passed away a couple years ago, he knew several rangers who helped on those investigations. He too also showed me what rangers told him were the areas they investigated. When you examine the map of their sweeps, they came close but for some odd reason, never touched the area Pacer and I found. At least not that I know about."

Chet looked at the map. He saw that Jack had marked the location he found the video. "It doesn't make sense."

Chet had previously explored the region of the large park where the fateful expedition took place. So had Hollis, Paul, and Brandon, familiarity and confidence of their locale were not an issue. The four men had hiked, camped and scouted the area twice before bringing an expedition to it. They even heard calls and whoops each time they visited. The four of them checked, double-checked, and triple-checked their agenda as to how the expedition would unfold, the approach they would take in hiking the trail-less mountain. Chet had a hard time believing he didn't lead authorities to the right location. It just didn't seem plausible. However, he wondered…

"I've also always wanted to know - how on earth did you pick that location? I mean it's way out there," Jack said.

"It certainly is," Chet said. "Actually both Hollis and Paul had heard for years about Bigfoot activity in and around that area of Oregon. Hollis said that his dad shared with him ancient Indian lore that had to do with Sasquatch in that region. Something about how the Indians and these creatures came to share and respect the land. The Sasquatch were supposed to watch over the local tribes, preventing bear and mountains lions from attacking members as long as tribesmen stayed out of certain mountains."

"That's pretty wild," Jack blurted.

Chet continued. "As for how we came to that particular site – Hollis's dad said the area that is now the south end of Hills Creek Reservoir was the location the Indian legends referred to. As you know, the lake is a man-made creation constructed and designed by the Army Corps of Engineers. And believe it or not, when we researched into the construction of the dam, a lot of Bigfoot stories emerged that centered on that southern region. Hollis found a story where three men went missing while on a surveying expedition. A few other people mysteriously disappeared during the construction; carelessness or drunkenness was cited as primary reasons for such things. We simply circled an area we thought was remote and hoped something would happen."

Alex sat mesmerized. "You said you scouted the area a couple times. Any activity?"

Chet nodded. "Yeah. Like I said, a few times we heard calls, whoops, heard knocks. It was great. The activity sealed the deal on going there with a larger group."

"That is amazing stuff," Jack chimed in.

Chet sat back in his seat. "My God, I haven't talked about any of that in ages." He laughed before casting a serious expression. "Can we watch that video again?" He sat up. "I want to see if there are any markers I may have missed that would lend credence to your theory, Jack. If I remember correctly, the rocks in that clearing had features that made it easier to identify what we wanted as a base camp."

"I photographed our hike pretty extensively when Pacer and I explored the area," Jack said. "I have the photos on my computer and laptop," he said turning away to retrieve his laptop bag. "They may prove better resources as they are better lit, and you can see elements of the landscape with greater clarity."

Chet edged closer to the end of his seat. "Yeah, I'd love to see those. Did you photograph all the encampments?"

"I did," Jack said as he powered up his laptop. "Here it is." Jack clicked the folder, and the images began to appear as thumbnails. He clicked a single image, and it came up bigger in a preview box. "Okay, I need to scroll down a bit."

Both Chet and Alex scooted in closer. They watched as Jack scrolled through the images slowly. Most of the shots looked indistinguishable: Trees upon trees.

"What's with all the forest shots?" Alex asked.

"Bushwhack," Jack said not taking his eyes off the screen. "There aren't any man-made trails up there."

"He's right. You're off the beaten path in that area. A couple feeder trails, some natural rain runoff lines in the landscape but certainly nothing that people would look and say – hey that's a trail," Chet said.

"All right," Jack said. "Here we go. These images are of the various encampments. We slated each one, not trusting that we could visually identify them when we returned home."

"Smart move," Alex said.

"This is Camp 1," Jack said.

"Brandon's camp," Chet said instantly recognizing the surroundings as if his mind dug out the memory from a long buried file.

The images revealed a clearing no more than thirty feet

across at its widest. A couple of blown down trees laid rotting, moss covering the rocks and felled trees.

"We found nothing here," Jack said before scrolling to another set of images. "But, you'll see what makes this site unique is the natural fire pit in the middle." Jack pointed to how a set of rocks broke through the surface, not touching at the top, creating a circular dip in the formation with two narrow cutouts acting as vents.

"Yeah that's right," Chet confirmed. "They used that, Brandon's group, to make a fire that night. Worked out great from what I recall."

"I found remnants of a fire in it. Soft gray goo and what appeared to be scorch marks on the rocks from a fire," Jack said as he scrolled through some pictures he took of it. "You can see from the photo it had been a while since someone last visited the site."

"How often have people gone here?" Chet asked.

"Not exactly sure when people started to travel there, but I guess somewhere above fifty have tried. How many are successful getting to the exact sites is up for speculation" Alex added. "Like I said, it's kind of a pilgrimage destination for some Squatchers."

"Hold on," Chet said with an abruptness. "So people have gone up there, but you're telling me the cops got it wrong in their investigation?"

Jack nodded. "Exactly."

"How's that possible? Why was this never followed up?" Chet asked, somewhat irritated.

"I don't think most of the people that explored the area put two and two together or knew if they truly came to the spots you had camped in," Jack answered. "Only a few have looked into your case like I have. I didn't get a chance to get up there until about two months ago."

"Again, not everyone who tried to reach that area had success," Alex added.

"Refresh my memory - how did you have success?" Chet asked Jack.

"Well, for one, we originally followed in the footsteps of what the investigators searched, and though we found some clearings, they didn't seem to match what your story offered. Then using the notes Pacer retrieved from Paul's ex-girlfriend, we map and compassed our way west. When we came to the new clearings, it felt right, seemed to match more closely what you had mentioned. For instance, this fire pit, you described it to the authorities, and they said they found a site that matched what you were talking about. I believe I found that site as well. But, this one here, the one we are looking at is a better fit, and it has trace evidence of a fire, unlike the other spot. I'll show you a picture of the ones the police discovered shortly. You'll see they appear alike but not quite."

"They all can look the same. There's hardly any real distinctions," Chet said, half defending the investigators.

"But enough that it made a difference… at least to us," Jack said. "You told police that your encampments were on rises in the landscape. However, one of your sites actually was in a slight dip, not a rise. I believe that led to some confusion," Jack said as he clicked to another picture.

"Wait!" Chet shouted with a burst of energy, half-ignoring Jack's claim about the landscape. He waved his hands. "Go back one."

Jack clicked back to the previous image. "Yeah, okay. You see something?"

Chet squinted as he peered into the image, a wide shot of the whole clearing. He even got on his knees to bring his face closer to the screen. "Can you zoom in closer?"

"Yes, I can. What do you see?" Jack asked.

Chet pointed to the middle left area of the screen. "In there. How close can you get?"

"Extremely close," Jack answered. "These are master files, the big ones."

Alex stood up and came closer. "What are we looking for?"

Jack clicked the area that Chet asked. A second later, the screen filled up with a small cluster of trees.

"No. Down a bit I think," Chet said.

Jack zoomed out some and began scrolling down. He stopped before Chet could say anything. His heart began to pound. Instantly perspiration started to seep along his forehead.

"Holy shit," Alex said with disbelief.

"Yeah," Chet said, as he peered in closer.

"No way," Jack said, his hand trembling on the mouse.

"Yeah way," Chet answered. "You were being scouted."

All three of them just stared at the dark object that stood partially obscured by a clump of trees several yards beyond the clearing. Pixelated but visible, the shape of a head, broad shoulders and two distinct shapes for arms were identifiable to them.

"That's not just some anomaly or play of shadow and light," Alex said wide-eyed and amazed.

"No, it isn't. That's a Bigfoot," Chet said. "And it looks like they are still in that region."

Jack let out a long exhale. "I can't believe I've never seen that. I wonder how many other pictures this thing is in?"

"It won't shock me if you find them in a couple others. You just have to look carefully," Chet said. "Like you said, bushwhacking; it's a lot of shots of trees. Your eyes glaze over seeing the same thing after a while."

For the next hour, the three of them scoured a variety of images from that area. Only two other pictures emerged that they could confidently say they spotted a Bigfoot. Other images looked to reveal some shapes but were dismissed as shadows, tricks of light or questionable enough that you couldn't go public with them without a high degree of skepticism.

"Let's check out the photos of what you believe is the true base camp," Alex said.

"Done," Jack said as he scrolled through to the images. "There's a lot more here since this is where I found the camera."

"Stunning that you found the camps," Chet said, still reeling in amazement at the images before him and that someone had actually discovered the expedition sites.

"I did. I'll even match video segments to the images I took so you can see they are the same. Like I said, the investigation never made it this far west that I ever read about. I know you said you pinpointed for them where to search but whatever duress you were under, you missed the mark, or they misinterpreted your information," Jack said before biting his lip and turning to Chet. "Sorry."

Chet waved him off. "I can't blame you."

Jack hovered the mouse over a few images, "And this is what I believe is base camp." He hesitated for a moment before finally clicking one. The picture opened and immediately Chet and Alex saw what Jack eluded too. Towards the center right of the image, two large stones protruded out of the ground. The lichen-covered rocks had two distinct features besides that they took up the majority of the clearing. The first rock closest in the frame rose up from the ground at a steep slant but had a flat top to it. The second, just beyond it and sticking out of the ground further, had a more jagged peak."

Chet pointed at the taller rock. "Hollis sat on that. He kind of liked being a king."

"That's right, and on the video, you see him sitting on it," Jack said.

Tears began to appear on Chet's face.

"You okay?" Alex asked seeing his friend try to fend off crying.

"I just need a minute," Chet mumbled, his voice choking.

"We can call it a day," Jack suggested.

Chet said no. "Just need a moment, then we plug ahead. I know one thing. We continue to look through your pictures; we'll spot another Sasquatch, maybe several more."

"Why? What makes you say that?" asked Alex.

"I don't know. Intuition," Chet said.

"So you're okay?" Jack asked.

"Got no choice really," Chet said. "I'm not going to start running away from my past now." He leaned back in his seat. "Maybe later, but not now."

Jack's somber face turned back to the screen. "Okay then, let's see what we have."

After examining a few dozen pictures, it netted them zero results. Chet made occasional remarks about the site and the conditions as he best remembered it. Jack shared more insight on his experience and the conditions he faced. The site had changed little, except moss had overtaken some of the fallen trees more so than Chet remembered.

Jack opened another image. Chet once again spotted something. He directed Jack to concentrate on the right-hand side of the frame.

"Something is in there, on the other side of the clearing," Chet said as he tapped lightly on the screen.

"I can't see anything," Jack said trying to look closer without zooming in on the spot.

"I see it. It's there," Chet said.

Jack zeroed in on the spot Chet pointed towards. As soon as the pixels cleared, a disturbing sight materialized.

"Oh shit," Jack said as he stared at a different creature. He knew instantly it was different. The build appeared more slight. This Bigfoot looked smaller in comparison to the others. The creature also had a different shade of coloring to it, more brownish-red than the earlier ones, which appeared darker.

"Can you call up the other one?" Alex asked, equally astounded by what he was observing on the screen.

Jack called up the best of the three they had discovered, and zoomed in, setting the two creatures side by side. "Oh shit, they are different."

"A lot different," Alex said.

"And it's not the lighting," Chet said.

"No, it's not," Jack added. "The shots are taken several hours apart. It was a cloudy day. The light remained pretty even the whole time."

"There's more around I'm sure," Chet said.

"You ain't kidding," Jack answered. "Check this out."

Jack moved the mouse a little to the picture's left and revealed another figure further in the distance. The pixelation made it tougher to see, but all three could plainly make out another humanoid like figure.

"Are you kidding me?" Jack said. "Those things tailed us the whole time we were there?"

"Apparently," Chet said. "It wouldn't surprise me if there were more but we just can't see them, or they were positioned elsewhere."

"Then why didn't they attack us?" Jack asked. "Why not us when we were clearly an easier target to take down?"

"I can't answer that," Chet said. "But they were there, and we have proof."

"I have a question, and I hope this comes out right," Alex said as he shuffled in his seat. "I don't understand why the Sasquatches attacked you guys? I mean... there are hundreds, thousands of sightings every year, and they aren't ever violent. It has always struck me as odd."

"I'll answer that," Jack interjected. "There are some violent Bigfoot reports. In fact, a number of missing camper cases have found ties to a possible Bigfoot abduction or worse, killing."

"Well, yeah, I've read some stories from way back, 19th-century stuff about how strange wild men like creatures drove families from their homes," Alex countered. "I've read the stories of remote fishing expeditions being haunted by some mysterious beings throwing rocks at cabins and hearing all kinds of howls. But, Chet's case is so unique."

Chet took a deep breath. "As you might imagine, I've had time to dwell on this. The best I could come up with was that our location allowed for it. Think about it. Most sightings occur near a road, a trail, seasonal road, field, some area where the person seeing the creature had easy access to leave the scene. Whether that person could run off or drive away, they all had the ability to exit in a straight line. My case is unique in that we were way off trail, up in a remote part of the park, no trails, no way to call for help. We were about as in the middle of nowhere as you could get. How much that played into what happened, I don't know. We didn't come as a threat, but they perceived us as one. Maybe we were in an area forbidden to anyone but them."

"There's actually a book on the subject that claims how Bigfoot have abducted people," Jack added.

"Really?" Chet said taken aback by the news.

"I heard the guy interviewed on *Coast to Coast* one night," Jack said. "I can't recall the book title but I'm sure if we searched the internet for it, we'd find it with no problem."

"It makes more sense that a creature would attack in an environment more conducive to its own favorability," Alex said. "But again, why attack if you posed no threat."

"We can't presume to think what a Bigfoot would consider a threat," Jack said.

"I don't know about that," Chet added. "We have to presume they are mammals and like most mammals, aside from humans, they rarely attack just to attack. What I experienced seemed calculated, coordinated. I have no explanation for the attack."

"Trespassing territory?" Jack suggested.

Chet shrugged. "I guess, maybe. But why not show themselves to you guys or any of the others who have supposedly tracked through that area?"

"And that's the great conundrum we circle back to, why?" Alex said, pausing as he looked at the computer screen of images. "You still want to go back Jack?"

Jack looked at both of them. His face remained stoic. "I want it now more than ever. Bigfoot is out there, and I want to bring the world undeniable proof."

"You don't think you have it with these pictures and the video?" Alex asked.

"No. It's never good enough. How many great pictures have we seen, films, video… all disputed at its best, mocked at worst," Jack said.

"You want to kill it?" Chet asked, his voice serious.

Jack took a moment. It wasn't like the thought never entered his mind as a solution to finally solving the great mystery about this legendary creature. "No. Not unless it threatens the team."

"And that's what we thought," Chet said. "It didn't work out."

Jack took a moment before standing up. "Between thermals, night vision gear, video, and photographic technology with far better sensors than ever before, if one of them comes close we'll get the proof we need." Jack walked over to his closet. Opening it, he pulled back some long jackets that hung down revealing a hunting rifle. "And we'll bring rifles. Each team will have at least one, if not more. It isn't something I'm high on, but we'll need to be armed."

"You've got the team?" Alex asked.

"I've got them," Jack said.

"And the equipment?" Alex asked.

"Some… but always could use more and better," Jack said.

"I know the guy who can take care of that," Alex said.

Chet dropped his head down and let out a huge exhale. "I know who you are going to say. My issue is that if you want me to come along, I don't want to make a circus out of it. I don't want my name dragged back into the news... no cameras, no bullshit commentary. If he comes, he comes alone, no camera crews."

Alex understood. He then revealed some news. "I spoke with him on that. He's intrigued. He also wishes you would change your mind."

"No," Chet said with an emphatic tone.

"Even if the money is right?" Alex prodded.

"The money doesn't mean shit," Chet said, his tone getting impatient.

"He told me to ask," Alex said backing off.

"And now you have his answer," Jack interjected. "But we will have cameras. I know where we can rent night vision and infrared gear. We'll have plenty of regular cameras and video equipment."

"That I understand and have no issue with," Chet said. "I just don't want to be some freak circus centerpiece for a television show."

"Not my intent," Jack said.

"And Sam wanted me to let you know, that if you refused his requests that he would still like to come along. He is, after all, serious about the subject. He may have a television show, but he also knows the importance of the research and proving the existence of Bigfoot," Alex said.

Jack looked towards Chet. "He could provide a lot of the latest technology."

"I understand," Chet said. "Are you ready to let him take command of your expedition?"

"He's not going to do that," Jack shot back.

"I know I've been away a while, but I can't imagine that when it comes to money and prestige, he's changed all that much. If he's fronting the cash and equipment, he's going to want his say, especially if he has the ego I suspect he has," Chet said.

"Then we'll have to work on an understanding. As far as I see it, I've done the legwork. Know where to go, have the footage, the pictures, all the preliminary information, and crew. And if I'm correct, I hope I have your support," Jack said feeling protective of his project.

Chet nodded. "You have my support."

"What of it Alex?" Jack asked.

"I can see what he says," Alex answered. "You're right in suspecting he'd want a say in things."

"He can have a say," Jack said. "I don't mind insight, but I'm not letting him hijack the project. It's not his show."

"Like I said, I'm sure you two can work out the details," Alex said.

"And don't forget, I'm not the centerpiece of this," Chet insisted. "The moment it becomes so, I'm outta there. I don't care if I have to solo it back. I am not the center of attention on this. And if I see cameras pointing at me in excess, I'll end my portion."

"I've given you my word," Jack said.

"I can set up a meeting to discuss the details, but one other thing," Alex said letting their eyes drift to him.

"What's that?" Chet asked taking the words out of Jack's mouth.

"I want in on this expedition too," Alex stated.

"I'm okay with it, are you okay with that Chet?" Jack asked.

"It sounds good to me. The more the merrier. As for Sam's part in all this, I'll listen to what he has to say."

Chapter 12

"Oh my God… really?" Corrine said. She glanced down at her grilled chicken salad shaking her head, still trying to process the news Chet just gave her. "Are you sure that's what you want to do? Really? To go back?"

After meeting at the bar, the two steadily developed a close relationship. Corrine dismissed Chet's past. Rather, she appreciated his compassion and his limitless ability to listen. She found comfort in his gentleness. She also believed every word Chet said about his innocence. As she told Betty, who remained somewhat skeptical, "the eyes don't lie, and he simply had nothing to do with their tragic deaths."

"If I don't go, I'll feel chained forever to this weight that hangs from me," Chet said. "Believe me, if I could, I would disappear from all this and start fresh somewhere far away. But this… this past, I have to see if I can shed it somehow."

Chet knew he could never erase people's judgments about him, but the more he thought about possibly exorcising the demons that haunted him, the more he craved to make the expedition happen. He looked at Corrine and could see the gleam of tears welling up in her eyes. "Don't you want to shed those nightmares?"

"What? By reliving it?" Corrine nearly shouted. "I can't go back into those woods. That area is too close for comfort for me."

"So living scared will suit you just fine?" Chet asked trying not to add an edge to his voice. He liked Corrine. She made him laugh. Yet, she had moments, dark moments that needed tending and caring for. Chet did that and didn't mind. The trauma she shared with him about what happened on her hiking trip weighed her down like an anchor as well. He watched how the color faded from her already ivory like skin, how her eyes seemed to sink into her face, her lips quiver almost as if possessed when those shadows of the past came back to plague her.

"Chet, what happens if they attack again? Aren't you afraid you're going to die?" Corrine asked.

"I'm dying now," he answered. He reached over and grabbed her hand. "So far you've been the only person who's given me any kind of lifeline of hope. You've listened to my concerns. I've had such a hard time opening up about some of the conflicting feelings going on. I'm always a brave face in front of others, but you… you've let me be vulnerable, unsure. You've helped me realize I need this expedition… And I think you need it too."

Corrine answered with a meek grin.

Chet continued. "And as much as you have meant to me these last two months, I still need to do this. I'm going to do it. I carried so much resentment in prison. It ate me alive. I began to learn to release it, but for as much as I learned to accept my fate, I could never take responsibility for the outcome. It wasn't my fault. I did nothing wrong. Yet all I ever heard was that I needed to accept responsibility in order to move on." Chet paused. "Of course I was found guilty because the law had to pin it on someone. I survived, but really, did I? I look at this expedition as a chance for a rebirth of sorts."

Corrine could only sit and listen. She could see the depths of his despair in the contortions of his face, the wrinkle in his brow and in the darkness that seemed to glaze his eyes whenever the subject of prison or the killings came up.

"Something inside is driving me back there," he continued. "At first, I didn't think I would have anything to do with this stuff again. Yet as soon as I saw the video Jack found and the pictures from his trip and hearing about your incident... I just need a way to cleanse myself of this dark cloud. Do you understand?"

Corrine nodded. "I do. You're braver than I am." She looked away. "I don't know if I have the strength."

Chet squeezed her hand. "And what? You have the strength to live frightened by your nightmares, terrified by a howl? You won't go back in the woods and experience one of the things you love doing most?"

"I'm afraid I'll die," Corrine answered, the words fumbling out of her mouth, tears following.

Chet let her hand go as he leaned back in his chair. "Honey, you're dying before me right now. The thing is... you know it. Every day this anxiety feeds off you, taking a little more of your soul. If you don't address it in some form, it will only eat at you more, and you'll disappear further into your own despair."

Corrine didn't respond, trying to pull herself together.

"I'll share something else," Chet said, his voice soft and understanding. "The other night, over at your place, I was awake while you tried to muffle your crying into your hands. I saw you sitting on the edge of your bed trying to keep it together. I know you don't want me to see that. I know you don't want to burden me with your pain, but it's okay. I can't speak for exactly how you feel, but I know I can empathize; sympathize with the turmoil you are suffering."

Corrine nodded, her eyes glazed, lips tucked into her mouth. She closed her eyes. "I'll go," she mumbled. "You're right. I won't be able to let it go unless I can confront my fears."

Chet nodded. "Okay."

"Besides, it'll be a hell of a lot cheaper than to pay some shrink thousands to come to the same conclusion," Corrine said half laughing while wiping a stray tear.

"They have their place, but look at me," Chet said, once again taking her hand. "I talked to one nearly every week for twelve years and I still occasionally see one, but in the end, it's the actions you take that moves you forward."

"I can't imagine how much that would cost," Corrine said.

"Too much," Chet said with a chuckle, then picked up his fork. "The foods getting cold, we should eat."

"Yes," Corrine said picking up her near empty wine glass. "And another one of these."

Chapter 13

Jack, Pacer, Alex, Avery, and Amy concentrated their eyes on a topographic map and a park map used by rangers identifying all the logging and seasonal roads in and around the Hill Creek Reservoir area. Using pieces from several unused board games, they plotted out encampments. Originally, Jack planned to drive to a certain point and hike in, but a small avalanche closed down the service road he wanted to access.

Jack informed them that Sam Ashford offered the use of several of his fifteen and sixteen-foot inflatable boats. They estimated the trip down the lake would take several hours. After stowing the boats, they would hike in and set up a camp at the base of the mountain they would climb the following day. The steepness of the slope would probably make the hike to their destination either a long day or two days depending on how people handled it.

"I want to make this the most extensive Sasquatch research event ever put together," Jack said keeping his excitement in check. "Looking at the list of people participating we have a lot of veterans coming out. As I mentioned before, Sam Ashford is joining us. I know some of you have either worked with or met him. He's agreed to provide several thermal cameras, as well as the boats and other amenities."

"We don't have any people on this expedition who don't believe Chet's story, do we?" asked Amy.

"No," Jack said. "I've vetted everyone involved. I know Carl Turk, and Harlan McDaniel have expressed doubts about Chet's story, but they didn't think he could kill all those people without leaving some kind of evidence. Besides, when they saw the footage, their minds changed."

"How many people are now involved with this trip?" Avery asked.

"As of this moment" Jack paused to count. "Fifteen. Three camps of five."

"That's a sizeable crew," Alex said.

"You think too much?" Amy asked.

"I do not," Jack said. "Pacer and I have been out there. There are plenty places to set up camps."

"Creepy places," Pacer added with a wink.

"Why would you say that?" Amy asked.

"Because in all honesty, it's a little creepy," Jack said. "There's logic to those feelings."

"And what's that?" Amy asked.

Jack looked at her with surprise. "Because each site has these stone works coming out of the ground that remind one of all the gloomy scenes from your favorite fantasy novels. Aside from patches of ground, most of these clearings are just rocky bald spots in the woods." He then pointed to the topographic map where little red circles dotted a section of the map.

Amy smiled then nudged him. "Okay, just keeping you on your toes."

A hard knock rapped on Jack's screen door. It was Chet. "Sorry for getting here late. I was talking to an old friend who might be interested in joining our little expedition."

"Who might that be?" Jack asked with mild surprise.

"Dr. William Westgaard," Chet said as he walked into the room.

Dr. Westgaard taught Zoology at the University of Oregon. He specialized in primates. His interest in Bigfoot extended all the way back to his high school days when, as a Boy Scout, he, Chet and some friends witnessed a Sasquatch while camping. People in the Bigfoot community knew Dr. Westgaard had an interest in the subject as he wrote about the phenomenon from time to time. He preferred a low profile on the matter as it tended to draw negative criticism and commentary from peers. Since he didn't make outwardly public proclamations on the existence of Bigfoot, his occasional writings generally asked questions or proffered scenarios for the creature's possible existence.

"That's great! How did you get him?" Jack asked.

"You've heard of him…" Chet said.

"I have. He's quiet on the subject of Bigfoot but not silent. I've read a few of his carefully worded opinions on the topic and how he believes in the possibility that such a creature might exist. How do you know him?"

"Longtime friend," Chet said. "Boy Scouts. We saw a Sasquatch together."

"What?" Alex exclaimed.

"How, where?" Pacer added.

"Northern California, late 80's. Bill, myself and this other scout Bobby Hartwell or something like that were collecting firewood along the shoreline of a lake when we spotted this tall, hairy creature walking along the opposite bank no more than two hundred feet away."

"That must have scared the shit out of you," Amy added.

"Actually, at first, we were more stunned and curious than anything. Then Bobby said it was a Bigfoot. That's when we nearly pissed ourselves," Chet said.

"No shit," Jack said.

"We stood frozen as we watched this great big thing meander its way along the wooded shoreline. It kept walking away from us. I don't think it ever saw us. If it did, it certainly didn't think we presented any kind of threat."

"How long did you watch it?" Amy asked.

"At least a minute, maybe two at most, before it disappeared back into the woods," Chet answered.

"That's some story," Alex said. "Did you tell the scout master or any of the adults?"

"We did," Chet said.

"What did they say?" Amy asked.

"They said we probably just mixed it up with a bear."

"Assholes," Pacer said with a shake of his head.

"Not really," Chet said. "That night, none of those adults slept. I remember not being able to sleep and looking out the tent. Those guys were all up, some standing, pacing and gazing into the woods. They knew what Bigfoot was all about."

"Yeah I guess you can't have them confirm it then wind up scaring the shit out of everyone in the troop," Jack said.

"Precisely," Chet shot back.

"So how did you convince the doctor to join us?" Jack asked.

"He always believed my story," Chet said. "I gave him extensive notes on what happened and made sure he took possession of all my research before I went away. Over the years, he came to visit, and we'd talk. He said if I ever had a desire to get back into researching that he'd help me out as best he could. I told him about this expedition: the goals, the crew, Sam Ashford's commitment and where we planned to explore. At first, he seemed a little reticent, but it didn't take long for him to agree."

"This is spectacular," Alex said.

"Only one caveat," Chet said. "You can't advertise his participation. He gets final say on any video usage of him."

"Done," Jack said.

"He wants to have a meeting to go over details, precise goals, gear available. He may have some advice on how to better set up a research agenda," Chet said.

"Zero issue," Jack said. "I think we'd all agree having a Ph.D. helping out with organizing the agenda is a positive step."

Everyone agreed.

Chapter 14

The alarm clock sounded. The long digital beeps shot into Chet's head like a nail from a nail gun. He whipped his body over on the bed and slammed his hand down on the cheaply made piece of plastic, nearly cracking the casing. Running his hand over his face and then through his hair, he turned and looked at Corrine's naked shoulders. He smiled thinking about the enthusiastic and rowdy sex they had just a few hours earlier. He loved the way she closed her eyes, ran her fingers nails across her own chest and moaned while she rode him on top. That thought got him to swing out of bed and stand up. Glancing at the clock, he saw it read 3:12 am.

Leaning over, he placed his hand on her shoulder and gave her a little push. "Hey, we gotta get up. It's time. Gotta get ready. Last real shower for a couple days."

Corrine stretched. "So soon. Didn't we just go to sleep?"

"It was your idea to have a last minute workout."

"You worked me too hard you big brute," she said opening her eyes and flashing him a lazy smile.

"Ready for a little hair of the dog then," Chet said as he walked towards the bathroom. "It might be the last time for a couple days."

"What… we can't make love in a tent?" she said, standing up slowly.

"We can but with the noises you like to make, we might attract more than just Sasquatches."

"Yeah, like you're the quiet one Mr. Oh My God, Oh My God."

Chet laughed. "Just trying to keep up."

"Shut up," Corrine said as she dragged herself into the bathroom.

Chet turned the shower on. The room soon began to steam up. "After you my lady."

"Thank you," she said.

"Your personal wash boy at your service," Chet said following her in as he cupped her bottom.

A caravan of vehicles turned off Willamette Highway and headed down a stretch of road towards the Hills Creek Dam. Still dark, but with the first hints of morning light casting a purplish-pink hue along the eastern mountain tops, the vehicles proceeded to a large parking area. Filing in one after the other, each car pulled into a slot in perfect synchronicity. In total, two cars and four SUV's pulled into parking spots; the SUV's pulling trailers of large inflatable boats and equipment.

Chet, Jack, and Alex got out and made sure all the cars appeared organized. Knowing they would go into the woods for several days, they wanted to make sure the parking of the vehicles looked good. They didn't want to attract any undue attention from the park service.

Walking up and down the line of vehicles, Chet was happy that everyone had complied with their request. He then walked over to two of the black Cadillac SUV's pulling the boats and watched Sam Ashford roll back the tarp on one of the trailers.

"Amazing the equipment you have," Chet said peering into the trailer full of small boxes packed with camera's, night vision goggles and thermal gear.

"You can thank my sponsors," Sam said. "They paid for most of this stuff."

Chet turned to see Bill walk up to them.

"Sam, this is my dear friend Dr. Bill Westgaard. Bill, Sam Ashford," Chet said introducing the two.

"I've seen a lot of your show," Bill said as the two shook hands.

"And I've read some of your work. It's good to have you along," Sam said. "I understand you're camera shy."

Bill smiled. "For the moment. I ask out of professional courtesy. It's not something the university would like to answer for."

"I understand," Sam said. "If this goes well, you might not have to worry about the university answering negative inquiries."

"Let's cross that path should we get to it," Bill answered. "What can I help you with?"

Chet gave Bill a light slap on the back. "I'll let you two get acquainted. I'm going to see how I can help Jack."

The sun still hadn't crested the distant peaks when the group pushed off from the boat launch and began their slow ride out into Hill Creek Lake. Jack and Chet estimated they had about a fifteen-mile ride to their landing site at Coffeepot Creek. Chet estimated it would take roughly two-plus hours to arrive at their destination. Once they brought the boats to shore and stowed them, the team would follow a service road before veering off and bushwhacking their way to the base of the mountain.

A light steady southerly wind created rippling waves over the entire lake. It also pushed straight into their faces, slowing their progress. With the load each boat carried, the engines couldn't propel them more than ten miles per hour.

Bill, Sam, Chet, and Corrine took the lead vessel and brought most of the food supplies for their three to four night outing. Veteran investigators Zachary Jacobs, Stan Garner, and Sam's cameraman Pete Solder piloted the boat carrying the rest of the food supplies and most of the backpacks. Alex, Carl Turk, and Avery manned the third boat, containing the rest of the backpacks and other miscellaneous gear. Behind those boats, Jeff Case, and Nathan Avent manned the boat with almost all the technical gear including the night vision equipment, while Jack, Pacer, Harlan and Amy protected the rear.

Chet and Sam conferred with Jack, over the radio and decided they shouldn't travel faster than about seven miles per hour unless the wind died down. They feared sapping the engines of energy. Even though they carried a spare battery for each boat, they didn't want to take a chance of overworking them. Sam preferred battery operated engines as they were generally quieter, making communication easier from boat to boat.

"Couldn't ask for better weather," Chet said feeling the constant cool breeze on his face. He held his hand on the rudder control arm and kept admiring the dark shapes of the mountains surrounding them, watching the subtle shift in light slowly reveal more and more detail of the surrounding area.

"And the weekly forecast is for little to no rain," Bill said.

Corrine laughed. "I trust a five-day Oregon forecast as far as I can throw it."

"Very true," Chet said. "However, if it holds, we'll have excellent weather for research."

"Certainly prefer not to get caught in any downpours with some of this gear," Sam added. "Let's hope the weather favors us."

"One never knows out here. You know how these mountains can create their own weather," Chet added.

"Look," Corrine shouted as she pointed to a couple Eagles off in the distance on the western shore.

The whole boat watched the magnificent creatures soaring high above the lake. Bill grabbed his binoculars while Chet radioed back to the other boats about the sight.

The large birds did a slow circular dance as if demonstrating how a screw turned. One of them suddenly dropped out of the sky like a stone straight for the water. The bird disappeared into the lake hardly making a splash before arising with a large fish clutched in its talons.

"That was awesome," Chet said with a loud whoop.

"Beautiful sight," Corrine added.

"Stunning," Sam followed, then got on his radio and asked if his cameraman, Pete Solder recorded it.

"You bet I did," Pete radioed back. "Lucky I happened to be shooting a little b-roll."

Part of the agreement Chet and Jack struck with Sam was that he could bring his own cameraman for documentary purposes but could only film Chet and Bill with their permission or backs turned and not be recognizable. Also, Jack negotiated partial rights to any documentary made from Sam's footage and vice versa for anything Jack created.

Another eagle dove down, appearing seconds later with a fish in its clutches.

Corrine glanced back at the other boats after hearing a few cheers. She could see how much delight the sight of the eagles brought to everyone. An ease flooded over her. She felt relaxed. For the first time in weeks, the tension that created stiffness in her shoulders suddenly disappeared. She turned to Chet, placed her hand on his knee and expressed her thanks for convincing her to come along. She hadn't realized just how much she missed seeing nature unfold before her.

The sun crested one of the lower eastern mountains and the day quickly began to warm. Large puffy white cumulous clouds evolved as if on cue from the sun's emergence. The clouds contrasted the still mostly dark silhouettes of the mountains ahead of them. Chet then noticed something a little odd: no fishermen. Usually, the lake hosted a number of boats, but he had yet to spot any. He radioed the others and asked if anyone had seen any kind of human activity on the lake. Only Harlan reported seeing a few fishermen early on, closer to the dam area, but since then nothing.

"Very weird," Chet said as he continued to scour their surroundings, hoping to see more activity.

"Just an odd anomaly," Bill said. "Besides, it's Wednesday morning, middle of the week, most people are working."

"I suppose," Chet said as he continued to scan the empty waters of the long lake.

The wind picked up more. The weather forecast said winds could gust to 20 mph. Chet could feel the engine working hard to keep a steady course. He had to hold a firm hand on the rudder to maintain a straight course. He asked Corrine to keep an eye out and inform him if any of the other boats struggled to keep in formation. Falling off course too much could easily find a boat drifting way behind and delaying their estimated arrival time at the cove.

"Over there," Bill said, pointing, his voice excited. "A Lenticular cloud."

"No shit," Sam said looking more keenly at it, pink hues accentuating the lower curving rim. "I haven't seen many but boy they certainly are weird looking things." Again, he radioed to his cameraman to make sure Pete recorded the scene.

"It looks like a giant white spaceship," Corrine said, captivated by the sight of the three-tiered, off white colored disc shape sitting between the peaks of two mountains to their southwest. "You can even see what look like lines defining the circular shape."

"That's the wild thing about them, that odd resemblance of a UFO," Chet said. "You've never seen one before?"

"Only pictures, a couple times on the news and sometimes on some hiking pages on Facebook but never in person," Corrine answered.

"It's only the second good one I've ever seen," Bill added.

The group of travelers marveled at the natural phenomenon. Several people started singing the theme to *Close Encounters* while others did *The Twilight Zone* bringing about loud laughs and cheering which they could hear echo around them adding to the surreal-ness of the scene.

While people continued to discuss the cloud, Chet noticed a landmark off in the distance. Using his binoculars, he checked it out then grabbed his radio to call Jack. "Packard Creek Campground two o'clock." He pointed in a southwesterly direction in line with the lenticular cloud. "You can see the open beach line. That campground has a sizable beach for swimming. The lake forks after we pass that. We stay left."

Jack picked up his binoculars, a larger pair with more magnification and peered off into the direction Chet mentioned. "It makes sense," he radioed back. "Just about halfway there. And straight ahead you can see the lake begins to narrow."

"That's right," Chet said. He glanced at his watch, confirming his estimation of time for reaching certain landmarks. "A little off," he said aloud to himself.

"What?" Corrine asked hearing Chet mumble.

"Just checking the time and our progress," Chet answered.

"How we doin' there Magellan?" she quipped.

"On course, but behind on time, thirty minutes maybe. The wind and choppy waters have slowed us down a bit," Chet noted. "We have a lot of day left." He shot her a reassuring smile to let her know he was happy she came along. She returned the grin as she slid her hand along his leg.

Bill caught the affection out of the corner of his eye. "Hey now… you're gonna need a room for that."

"I guess a tent will have to do," Chet said as he gave Corrine a wink.

"Good, now I know to pitch mine on the opposite end of camp. I don't want to hear all that," Bill said as he covered his ears.

"We'll try to keep it to a low roar," Chet said.

The radio crackled. "Eastern shore, ten o'clock, looks like two bears," Jack said from his boat that trailed Chet's by about a hundred yards.

Corrine spotted them first, despite not having binoculars.

"We're having a banner day with the wildlife and natural

phenomenon," Chet said, spotting the adult black bear and its smaller counterpart, a cub.

"Wonderful," Sam added, observing through his binoculars. He turned back to see his cameraman shooting footage of the scene.

"Hopefully we won't run into any of that while hiking," Bill said, also spotting the two animals. "Still, quite stunning to see. If we had time, getting a closer look would be interesting."

"Yeah, I'm good from here," Corrine said. "I had a close encounter with a bear once. No thanks."

"What happened?" Bill asked.

"Hiking," Corrine said. "Near Crater Lake. A weekend hike. Five of us were just going along a trail… we came to a bend and BAM, there it was, this Black Bear."

"Was it big?" Chet asked.

"It was big enough. As to exactly how big, I couldn't tell you, I was just hoping the thing wouldn't think of us as a threat."

"What did you do?" Bill asked.

"This guy Roger had bear experience, and he said we should gather together, and do a little swaying. He said bears have bad eyesight, and that might just make him move on, especially if it thought we were of a formidable size."

"That's right," Chet said. "Did it work?"

She nodded. "It took a minute, but the bear eventually turned around and disappeared into the woods. We stood there for another couple minutes just to make sure. Roger followed it as far as he could using a small pair of binoculars to track it."

"Wow, that's some story. How close were you to it?" Bill asked.

"A hundred feet maybe. I was flush with fright. That kind of bravery has never been my strong suit. I can stand up and talk to a crowd of people, sell a product to strangers but bears, mountain lions… not my thing."

"Don't sell yourself short," Chet said.

Corrine acknowledged his words, then went back to watching the bears meander along the shoreline. The creatures paid no attention to them, never once looking their way. The mother bear twice slapped at the water, but nothing came of it. A couple minutes later, the bears turned towards the forest and vanished from sight.

"How about you Sam? You've spent a lot of time out in the wilderness… any bear encounters?" Bill asked.

"Nothing like what Corrine shared. But I've seen several. The closest one was while shooting an episode in northern California. We spotted a grizzly about five hundred feet away, across a river. We had the high ground. No one moved once we spotted it. It never appeared to notice us. We watched it, filmed it for about ten minutes before it walked away," Sam answered, recounting the story as if performing a voiceover. "All my other sightings, probably about five, they've been well off in the distance. Still, any footage you can get works great as a teaser for the show."

The lake began to narrow. The mountains loomed bigger as the landscape closed in. The tall Douglas Firs that dominated the landscape began to look much larger. Before, many looked like spikey green toothpicks but now, with more detail revealed, they all could see just how tall and majestic the trees appeared, painting themselves all over the sloping mountains.

"Did any of you guys ever see that movie, *The Land that Time Forgot?*" Chet asked.

"No," Corrine said.

"Long time ago," Bill said.

"This kind of reminds of that," Chet said.

"I can see that," Sam chimed in.

"I'm afraid to ask," Corrine said before quickly following up her own words. "No, I'm not. What is it?"

"It's a science fiction movie from the 70's," Chet said. "This group on a submarine find themselves in a strange place loaded with dinosaurs. Somewhat cheesy, but entertaining enough."

"Oh great, dinosaurs," Corrine replied with a shake of her head. "Let's hope we don't accidently run into any of those."

Another hour passed. The winds died down to an occasional soft breeze. The waters flattened. All remained quiet except for the occasional white noise of chatter and the hum of the electric engines. Entering through the narrower part of the lake mesmerized the onlookers. Most had never traveled to this more remote part of the reservoir. Only Chet had traveled the lake by boat to this end, twice. Jack and Pacer drove down the service road when they explored the area as most seekers of the fabled Bigfoot site had. However, due to a small avalanche on National Forest Road F 2118, that made it impassable for the foreseeable future.

The riders basked in the warmth of the early September sun now rising steadily above all the surrounding peaks. The clean blue water reflected the clouds above like a heavenly mirror. The silence of the surrounding wilderness hypnotized them all into a relaxed stupor. Chet popped on his dark tinted sunglasses and simply scanned back and forth across the serene green mountain landscapes before him.

Slicing through the silence came a screech that echoed all around. Everyone jerked in complete surprise to the piercing sound. Heads turned, binoculars and eyeballs tried to spot the source of the other-worldly sound.

"What the hell was that?" Corrine asked, her eyes darting all over.

Chet didn't know. "Wasn't an owl, hawk or eagle that I've ever heard."

"It wasn't that," Bill said.

Jack's voice broke over the radio asking if anyone spotted the source of the sound.

"Nothing here," Chet radioed back. "Anyone see anything there?"

"Not even sure where it started from," Jack answered.

"Is it possible it was an elk or maybe even a mountain lion?" Sam chimed in.

Several head nods gave the thought some credence. Though rarely seen, mountain lions weren't an uncommon species to the region. Chet had only seen one in all his years in the wilderness, and it was a good distance away from his vantage point.

"Kyle said he saw two while doing his hike that he wrote his book on," Corrine said. "He said they can have a bone-chilling call, high pitch shriek like."

"It's the best answer we have yet," Bill said.

Jack then radioed. "Chet a few of us wanted to ask if that was anything like what you may have heard when you reported hearing all the calls that surrounded your camp before the attack?"

Chet answered promptly. "No. Nothing like that. If we hear what I heard, mountain lions will sound like purring kittens."

No responses came back.

Silence once again overtook the group as larger, more ominous looking clouds rolled into view. A few minutes later, cloud cover blotted out the sun. They could feel the immediate impact as the temperature cooled instantly. Chet held firm onto the arm of the rudder and just kept course. He glanced at the map he had on a small clipboard then along the continuing nondescript shoreline. It wouldn't be long before they spotted their destination.

"That's it," Chet said pointing to his left where a section of low-lying land, mostly filled with small scrub and a noticeable beach line, jutted out from the steep mountain faced landscape.

"You sure," Corrine asked rhetorically.

"Absolutely," he returned. "We'll see a small cove coming up just beyond the lip in the land." Chet picked up his radio and reported his finding to the others. He could hear soft cheers as the several hour's long ride on the lake was now finally ending. Chet began to steer his boat closer to the shore. For good measure, he increased the speed of the engine a touch. From the middle of the lake, the mountains didn't appear as ominous as they began to now. Chet nodded. He hadn't forgotten. Over twelve years had passed, but the same feelings he had about these mountains and what lived in them came rushing back. He choked back the adrenaline that exploded in his mouth and throat. He glanced at the other boats and watched the expressions on people's faces as the steep slopes before them revealed more of their precipitous grade.

Chet guided his boat past a section of beach that made up the lip of land. A small cove opened up and in moments, they could all easily see the service road that ran along the shoreline of the lake. Looking up, Chet and the others could see that a few gray clouds replaced the white puffy ones that had dominated most of the sky earlier. A few rumbles of worry sounded hoping it wouldn't rain.

Chet turned back to see that all the boats tightened up their formation. "Let's head for that open beach," he shouted as he pointed to the barren shoreline just across from the opening of the cove. "We'll pull ashore there and assemble."

When the boats came to shore, a nervous excitement ensued as the members of the expedition moved about like ants on a picnic blanket as they gathered equipment and camping gear. Alex and Jack oversaw making sure the crafts were covered and hidden away from plain sight. The Forest Service didn't often butt their nose into the comings and goings of hikers and campers, however, when large groups entered into an area, they often wanted a heads up. The problem with notifying the Forest Service was that they sometimes denied access or would fine people for violating any number of restrictions. They also protected the interests of logging companies and didn't need any protestors sneaking into those lands through the park. Also, Bigfoot expeditions didn't make the list of activities they wanted trekking through their forests. What Chet, Sam, and Jack knew was that if you were discreet and respectful with your group, and your belongings, the Forest Service generally looked the other way. Next to actually running into one of them, the group knew they could keep all their stuff low key, neat and out of sight.

"So, how far do we walk today?" Bill asked Chet.

"Well," Chet said as he gazed at the two looming landmasses that rose up on either side of them. "We'll follow the service road that cuts between these two peaks for a bit, five to seven miles, it goes a little uphill, but it's easy walking. We should make good time before we have to leave the road and walk along a creek for about another mile. The terrain gets uneven in there. That'll slow a big group down."

"That's right," Jack added as he entered the conversation. "We'll then come to a point where the land rises up quickly on two sides. We'll split the middle and take that route. There's what appears to be a natural run off trail we can follow. The trick is finding it."

"Exactly," Chet concurred. "That's how we came in all those years back. We should probably pitch camp at the base of that ascent and then start fresh tomorrow. We'll need the rest for sure…it's a tough climb."

Once off the service road, the group hiked over a mile, cutting through some scrub and underbrush they knew they would encounter. The expedition pitched camp along the banks of a fast moving stream that ran into Coffeepot Creek, which in turn flowed into the lake. The small clearing gave them a great view of the mountain they needed to scale. The initial upslope didn't seem too bad, but they could all see how the mountain straightened itself out, and the climb would become steep. The dark greens of the tall Douglas Firs above them cast a foreboding feel compared to the brush and scattered cedars and hemlock trees that dominated the lower elevations.

"It's going to be a tight fit with all these tents," Chet said to Sam, Bill and Jack who began organizing the night vision gear, recording devices, walkie-talkies and batteries to operate it all. "Might even have to machete a few small trees and bushes to fit everyone in."

"Then I nominate you to oversee that," Jack said not wanting the task of organizing a base camp.

"Second," Sam added.

Bill shrugged. "Sorry old friend but I third it."

"Aren't you guys just so sweet," Chet said before turning and walking towards the assemblage of tents.

Chet assisted where he could with tents then asked Amy, Corrine, and Pacer to start collecting kindling wood and fashion a fire pit. He pointed to where several sizable boulders peaked out of the ground, creating a small rise in the landscape. He thought that would be the best place to make a fire. The placement of the fire pit also split the camp in two, making the area a natural meeting ground. Chet asked others, as they finished with their setups, to look for larger dried branches to help keep the fire burning strong into the night. Within an hour, the entire camp stood ready, and a fire began to crackle.

Chet ducked into his tent and unrolled his sleeping bag, which revealed his shotgun. He reached into his backpack and took out a box of shells. He then loaded five rounds into the weapon. He knew this act broke his probation and could send him back to jail, but for this expedition and its purpose, he wasn't entrusting others with taking care of his safety. With the weapon loaded, safety on, he placed it underneath his sleeping bag.

Corrine popped her head into the tent. "How we doing? Everything okay?"

"It's all good," Chet said as he turned towards her and stepped out of the tent. "Just needed to set up the bedroll and stuff."

She gave him a quick peck as he exited. "I left yours, wasn't sure if it was my place to set your stuff up."

Chet appreciated the gesture, placing his hand on her cheek and lightly running his fingers across her soft skin. He mentioned he was going to bring a shotgun but didn't know how much stock Corrine put into it. He wasn't worried about her and weapons as she had her own gun license and owned a handgun. He did wonder if she worried about *him* having one.

"How are we looking?" Chet asked Harlan who happened to be the person closest to his tent when he exited.

"I think we're good. A couple people have already started to put together meals. We should be ready for that in a half hour or so," Harlan replied.

"Good, I'm hungry," Chet said. "We'll get everyone fed then have a meeting about how tonight and tomorrow will unfold."

"I heard people asking if we're going to do any calls tonight," Corrine said emerging from out of the tent.

"We're here, we might as well make the most of it," Chet said. "Listen, I'd be happy for some kind of results... the sooner, the better." He looked up the slope of the mountain. A cloud passed in front of the late day sun and deep shadows engulfed the camp. The trees around them lost all color, shifting the scene into varying degrees of dark. Chet felt a chill as he gazed at the tall, still sentinels that surrounded them. He peered into the woods and could feel the impending night coming upon them. He thought again about making calls. He

knew it didn't matter if they did or not. *They know we're here.*

Darkness crept across the camp as the sun disappeared behind the mountains. A chill set in with the onset of deepening shadows. Looking to the sky, a softer darker hue appeared, and the clouds began to exhibit touches of pink and purple in them. Members of the expedition changed into vests or light jackets. The fire crackled louder and brighter in the dimming light.

"Is Chet okay?" Jack asked Corrine as she stirred a small pot over the fire.

"Yeah why?" she answered keeping her eyes on the pot, watching little streamlets wisp their way up into the air.

"He's been awfully quiet since the sun set behind the mountains," Jack said, glancing over to Chet who stood leaning against a tree, staring into the woods towards the path they would take in the morning.

Corrine felt defensive but tried to conceal it. "Look around. It's getting dark; we're closing in on the place where it all changed his life. He spent over twelve years in prison for a crime he didn't commit. He's probably reflecting… processing. Let him have his moment. I wouldn't be concerned."

Jack nodded, remained quiet for another minute as he looked over the darkening surroundings. "You think he's…" but before he could finish his question a loud tenor-pitched wail broke the silence. The sound echoed and hung in the air for a few seconds bouncing around camp. Stunned by the sound, many turned to look for the source of the call.

"Are you fucking kidding me," Jack yelled in surprise seeing that Chet had brought his hands up to his mouth to give out a big screech

Chet turned, surprised at the reactions on people's faces to his scream.

"We usually give notice before doing that," Jack said with a none too pleased laugh under his breath. He turned to the rest of the group. "If anyone has to change cause you soiled yourself, you can blame Chet, he seems to have forgotten protocol."

Chet made his way back toward him and Corrine.

"Sorry about that. Something just came over me and I let one go," Chet said.

"Yeah, I'm sure you're not the only one to have let one go," Sam added.

Off in the far distance, a return howl echoed, faint, but distinct. A guttural call, one made with some depth from the diaphragm. The sound lingered for a call that came from far away. It only confirmed what Chet knew already.

"Tell me that was a coyote," Corrine said knowing it wasn't but hoping for the best.

"That wasn't any coyote," Sam said. He looked towards Jack and Chet. "Weapons?"

Chet took a moment, almost as if he wanted to savor every last vibration of the call no matter how faint. He turned his head slow, inspecting his surroundings with a scout's observant discipline. "Yes. It isn't a bad idea."

Chapter 15

Two people stood watch at either end of the camp. Both held rifles. Harlan held a position towards where the group had entered from the road. Chet stood a post facing the woods they would head into come first light.

Chet stared into the darkness in front of him. He'd gotten used to seeing in the dark. Years of staring at the ceiling in his cell in the middle of the night, he knew every crevice, nick, and line that wove itself across his tiny rectangular universe. After a while, he could actually see where the painters applied thicker and thinner coats as well as brush strokes along the trim areas.

Staring into the dark of the woods, he could discern its depths. The outline of the dark trees soon revealed detail, in the bark. Looking past the branches that hung off the firs like heavy arms, he could see the spacing between the trees. He knew the distance from one to the next. He sat dead still, only shifting his eyes in little measures. If a Sasquatch were out there, he would spot it.

Chet waited patiently and remained still, like a snake ready to strike. He felt the beasts were out there just beyond his sight. That call earlier they all heard - it was a signal. He'd heard it before. The memories, once thought lost, came rushing back. His expedition group from over a dozen years earlier had camped not far from where this current one set up. They had made calls as well, and he now remembered how a faint call from off in the distance echoed softly in the air. Yet then, no one knew what to make of the sound. Some debated it was a coyote, others some kind of cat, while others wondered if it was a Sasquatch. A consensus never came up, so the questions about it faded into other conversations.

Even he remembered not thinking much about it at the time but now… now he knew. With that thought, he clutched his shotgun with more force. *It's just a matter of when.*

Jack, Sam, Pacer, and others continued to talk about the strange, shrill, distant call. The laughter and relaxation that had buoyed the expedition earlier dissipated into everyone paying attention to any noise happening outside the camp's perimeter.

Chet heard their nervous chatter and wanted to reassure them that all was fine, but he couldn't lie to them that way. *Best to keep quiet.* He knew better, he felt it in his being that Bigfoot, a number of them, were already aware of their presence. He also knew the creatures wouldn't show themselves this close to the lake, *too easy for the expedition to escape.* No, if they were going to reveal themselves, they'd wait until the whole group found themselves deep in the forest. He wondered again if he should say something. *No.*

The crackling of footsteps on the forest floor alerted him that someone approached. His body tensed for a moment, his grip around the shotgun becoming firmer.

"Hey, how you making out?" Corrine asked, her voice smooth. She ran her fingers along his shoulders before she used her nails to give his head a soft playful scratch.

Chet did enjoy her gentle touch, as a few pleasurable goose bumps rippled over his body. "Doing well. I can hear that people are still a bit uptight about that call."

Corrine sat down close to Chet, rubbing her body up against his to get cozy. "Yeah, a bit, but I think it's finally beginning to fade."

"How are you doing?" he asked, nudging his body next to hers. He had developed a great affection for Corrine. Her reciprocity of feelings and affection was far more than he could have asked for coming out of jail. He wondered if Corrine latched onto him as a security blanket of some sort.

He helped her through her issues with his patience and understanding. Subsequently, her middle of the night panic attacks had subsided tremendously but not completely.

Chet felt that she now worked on him, easing his tension, and insecurities about having the label 'convict' attached to him. He hadn't given the 'convict' label much thought in prison, only knowing he was innocent of all crimes. Yet when released, he found himself in odd situations talking about his life... how does one account for twelve years behind bars? It didn't matter what he thought, perception dictated the stereotypical images of the label, convict. Corrine soothed those uncomfortable moments, helped him adjust to that unforgiving reality. To say he didn't have any resentment or anger towards those feelings only meant he was lying to himself. She helped him accept those feelings and begin to move past them.

Chet liked the way Corrine snuggled close to him and gently ran her fingertips up and down his inner thigh. He tried to hide the pleasure but couldn't. He heard her giggle a soft purr. Then he felt her soft breath blow into his ear.

"I'm going into our tent," she cooed. "Wake me if I fall asleep. I want you before we head up this mountain." She then kissed his cheek, got up and walked back towards camp.

"Anything?" Bill asked as he approached Chet about twenty minutes after Corrine left his side.

Chet had barely moved during his entire watch, his eyes peering into the woods, ever scanning, waiting to see something. "Nothing," he replied.

"Get some sleep," Bill said as he perched down next to Chet with his own rifle.

"Sounds good," Chet responded. Sleep tried to overtake him several times, but he mustered enough self-discipline to stay awake and diligent. He stood and felt the stiffness in his leg muscles from remaining in one position too long. It took a minute to regain his balance. He shook each leg to awaken it and lightly pounded his quadriceps with his fists.

"Better?" Bill asked watching Chet get his act together.

"My advice is to move more than I did," Chet said as he slung his weapon back around his shoulder. "Wake me as soon as you see first light. I want to scout the path ahead before we all go in – see if I can spot anything unusual."

"Why? You think something's out there?" Bill asked.

Chet hesitated to answer. He knew something lurked in the dark just beyond his vision. If anyone could handle the truth about his intuition, Bill could, he thought. Bill was an expert, a professional in his field of research. He didn't come out for a camping trip. "I'm almost certain of it," Chet answered.

Bill didn't flinch, but he felt a shiver run through his body at Chet's assured words. He only waited a second to answer but felt as if he answered from a vacuum. "Dangerous?"

"Not yet," Chet said, sure of his answer. "We could easily escape them from this location. They want better odds than that."

Bill thought Chet's answer rather surprising. "You're giving these creatures a lot of credit."

Chet didn't flinch in his answer. "They were able to send me away for over a decade to rot in prison. They get all the credit they want."

"Sorry," Bill said, feeling he may have insulted Chet.

"Don't be," Chet shot back. "Be alert. The difference between then and now is we know they are out there, and we're ready for them."

"You got it," Bill answered.

"Good night, and don't forget to get me up before the others."

Chet pulled back the flap to the tent. Corrine had left it unzipped so he didn't have to fiddle with it in the dark. He crouched and slid in. Corrine lay asleep on top of her sleeping bag wearing a pair of shorts that ran up high exposing much of her thigh. Chet smiled. He liked her long, strong legs. He slowly cupped the top part of her thigh near her buttocks then ran his hand along her side, tracing her breasts with a gentle touch. He saw her stir then open her eyes.

"Hi," she cooed.

He leaned in gave her a soft kiss on the lips. "Sleep," he whispered.

She nodded with a smile and nestled herself back into slumber.

Chet grabbed a blanket, unrolled it and covered her. The tent had a nice warmth to it but knew a chill could overcome the area at any moment. Looking at his watch, he figured he might get four hours sleep, if lucky. Still, he felt comforted by the idea of anything more than three. Lying there, he dimmed the LED lamp that hung in the center of the tent. In the dim light, he stared at Corrine's peaceful face as she slept.

"Psst," came the sound again and again until Chet stirred, sat up, looked towards the entrance of the tent to see an exasperated Bill looking at him.

"Any day sunshine," he whispered. "You wanted up before anyone; well… it's that time."

Chet nodded, told him to wait a minute, shook off the cobwebs in his head and began to change his cotton shirt into two wicking ones. He glanced over at Corrine. She remained asleep yet instead of the sexy angelic girl he fell asleep looking at, she now resembled a hot mess, hair everywhere, mouth open, snorts of snoring popping out and her body sprawled out, one hand leaning up against the tent's side. Chet couldn't help let out a chuckle at the sight. She didn't stir. He looked at his watch. The camp had another hour to sleep before they needed to break things down and get going.

Stepping out of his tent, shotgun over his shoulder, the scent of the trees filled his senses, refreshing and familiar. The temperature felt unseasonably warm, he hoped it wasn't a prelude to rain. It was still dark, but looking straight up towards the east, the hue of the new day's light began to take hold.

"What's the plan?" Bill asked.

Chet turned to see his longtime friend looking tired. "For one, you should try to get a quick nap. It would seem everyone still has another hour or so to sleep."

"I'll be fine," Bill said as he fought a yawn.

"Yeah, I can see that," Chet shot back.

"Again, what's the plan?" Bill asked.

"I want to scout out a trail," Chet said staring in the direction of the woods he wanted to head into.

"I'll come with you," Bill said.

"Get some sleep. I can manage."

"Sorry," Bill said having none of it. "A one-hour nap will be worse. If I try to get up from that, it'll just feel like someone pounded my head with a hammer."

Chet knew exactly what he meant: One-hour naps after being up late were worse than just staying up. "Okay then, follow me," he said without hesitation, turned his headlamp on and started to walk towards the thick of the woods.

Heading into the forest, darkness engulfed everything around the throw of his headlamp's light. Chet walked with purpose, his steps strong as he moved along in the trail-less woods without hesitation.

"You know where you're going?" Bill asked trying to hide his nervousness as Chet continued to walk at a brisk pace in the dark.

"You worried?" Chet asked as he made his way up the steepening slope.

Bill thought for a moment. No need hiding it. "A little."

"Good," Chet shot back. "It's what'll keep the edge on and keep you alive."

Bill let his words sink in. "You seem pretty certain these creatures are going to make their presence known."

Chet stopped. He didn't look back at Bill, just waited for him to catch up. "I'm preparing for the worst."

"Why?" Bill asked stopping a step behind him.

Chet felt like snarling but didn't. "Because I've seen the worst, and none of you have any real idea what that might entail."

Bill felt the weight of Chet's words and took heed of them. "You're right. None of us know what you know."

"And if I come off too intense as we get closer, it's just to keep everyone else on edge, because the loosey-goosie approach isn't going to save any of us if we do run into any kind of trouble." Chet took another breath. "I know for some folks this is some special kind of infamous celebrity outing in the woods with the hope of hearing or even seeing a Bigfoot. I'm telling you, they already know we're here. What they do now is another matter altogether."

"What exactly are we doing right now?" Bill asked wanting to deflect the tension.

"Looking for a game trail of some sort, or a natural water run off," Chet said. "Most never notice them. They are subtle, but when I came through this area, I saw them. I'm sure Jack and Pacer followed them. All woods have them. They can shift over time, but they don't become abandoned unless the environment is drastically changed or the food source dries up. Neither of those conditions looks like they have happened here."

"How much longer do you think?"

"I'm giving it another fifteen minutes," Chet answered.

Bill took a deep breath. "Okay captain, lead the way."

Corrine spotted Chet and Bill emerge from the woods. She gave a happy shout, alerting the others who had already started to break down the camp. Jack, Amy, Sam, and Harlan approached with concerned looks.

"What?" Chet said noticing their expressions. "I mentioned that I wanted to see if could spot out a trail that would make getting up the mountain easier."

Jack and Sam didn't buy his explanation so easily, their faces tight with aggravation.

"You could have said something last night," Jack said.

"Yeah, like a reminder of some kind," Sam added.

Chet didn't appreciate the accusation of wrongdoing coming his way, but he hadn't reminded any of them except Bill and Corrine as to his intentions. "Sorry, my bad," Chet said as he wondered if he had mentioned his intent earlier.

"Fine enough," Sam said, still holding himself stiff. "Did you find anything?"

"I did," Chet answered. "About a quarter of a mile up, maybe a little more, there's a game trail, almost looks like an old trail that may have been used a long time back. It heads up. I think we should follow it."

"Sounds good," Jack said.

"How long before you think we can head out?" Chet asked.

"Give it an hour and I think we can be on our way," Sam answered.

"How long do you think it'll take to get to the location?" Amy asked, looking less Goth and more girl next door with her hair pulled back in a single ponytail, no makeup, no piercings and wearing a baseball cap.

"Depends on the pace and the fitness of people," Chet said. "A fit crew gets there in seven or eight hours. I look at this group and think nine to ten, but it depends. Either way, we should get to our destination before nightfall."

"We allotted the whole day to get there, so if we're early, all the better," Jack said.

Chapter 16

Many hadn't expected the steepness or length of the climb. They were all briefed on it, but the reality spoke a different language than their perceptions envisioned. Most Bigfoot expeditions didn't require long bushwhacking hikes into little traveled or unknown regions. The longest hike many of the participants had ever done ranged around five miles in length on well-preserved trails. Hiking through a thick forest with little recognition of a trail and always uphill, wore on many of them. With a three hundred and sixty degree view that seemingly never changed - patches of thick ferns, moss covered rocks, downed trees and looming Douglas Firs reaching up to the sky - pangs of claustrophobia began to grip at a few people. Several times, the expedition had to stop so people could catch their breath. Anxiety rushes overcame some who had never experienced deep woods bushwhacking. Others clamored for more breaks because their legs sang with pain and exhaustion.

Chet felt exasperated by the slow pace. He glanced at his watch. It was just after five when they arrived at a small clearing, nearly ten hours since they broke camp. Another two hours and it would start getting dark. They hadn't made it to their destination. The topographic maps Sam, Pacer, and Jack possessed didn't indicate many clearings, except for those noted around the summit region. The three of them conferred on their location and estimated they still had another hour, maybe two, before arriving at their destination.

Entering the clearing brought a certain amount of relief and joy to the expedition until crewmembers found out it wasn't the intended site. Most fell to the ground exhausted.

A quick vote made it abundantly clear no one wanted to continue on.

"I guess this is camp for the night," Bill said, his shirts soaked with sweat. Not the fittest of people, though by no means obese, Bill felt he lost those twenty pounds he was trying to shed. "Tell you what," he said to Chet while dropping his pack onto the soft soil. "I'll sleep well tonight, Bigfoot or no Bigfoot."

Chet looked at his worn out friend; the shoulders slumped, matted wet hair caked to his skull and began to laugh. "You look like hell."

"I feel like I just finished hiking to the gates of it," he shot back, then sat on the ground and leaned against his pack.

"Don't get too comfortable, we still have to set up camp," Chet said. He then turned his attention towards where the majority of the expedition had settled. "Any of you lightweights up for a couple calls later this evening to see if there're any signs of life?"

Before the fullness of night surrounded the expedition, two fires flickered strong. Chet surveyed the area, examining how the various exposed rocks rose from the ground. He began to think about how he may have misguided authorities to the wrong location. He studied the grounds further, walking slowly, first around the periphery of the camp, then over the undulating rocks that took up much of the opening before stepping several strides into the woods.

"You okay?" Corrine asked, having asked Amy to take over the cooking so she could speak to Chet.

"A little disappointed I guess," he answered, looking towards the ground.

"Don't be," Corrine said, running her well-trimmed fingernails along his back. "These people don't know what a hard bushwhack is. Hell, that kicked the crap out of me, and I've done a couple."

Chet just nodded and continued to stare into the forest.

Sam came walking up. He made no bones about his incoming presence. "How far off course do *you* think we are?" Sam had never investigated this area. He outlined plans to visit, but the television show didn't want to lay out the money in liability insurance for a location so remote, let alone a crew fit enough to get to the place. He trusted Chet's instincts more than Jack's map and compass skills. Sam had trusted his instincts his whole life, and it served him well. Now, he would go with whatever Chet felt about the current location.

Chet looked out towards the direction they needed to head. "Two miles, maybe three. You can see just ahead how the bottoms of the trees even out more. The elevation stabilizes for a bit before one more ascent. It should take us roughly an hour to get to in the morning. Then all the other camps are within fifteen to twenty minute walks at most."

"Sounds good then… not too far off the agenda," Sam shot back, feeling better. "Jack thinks further."

"We can split the baby," Chet said. "Either way, we are headed in the right direction. I can feel it. It's like I'm being directed to it."

Sam and Corrine stood silent as they let his words sink in. Both wondered what he truly meant. Corrine reached out to grab Chet's hand.

"Thank you," he whispered to her.

Sam tipped his brown brimmed hat and shot them both a smirk. "I'll let the two of you have your moment."

Chet said nothing. He just kept a steady, silent gaze into the woods. A minute later, he turned to Corrine and placed both hands softly on the sides of her face, leaned in and kissed her deeply. He felt her hands slowly wrap around his back and draw him in closer to her. Slowly they both went to the ground, dipping behind a fallen tree and began to press their bodies tighter against each other, their kisses becoming deeper, wetter and more passionate.

"Wow! What brought that on?" Corrine said while running her fingers along his cheeks.

"Your beauty and an excess of energy that needed to be let out," Chet said with a breathlessness that indicated he wasn't finished.

Corrine smiled wide. "I felt all that energy press against my leg."

"It wants to do more than that," he whispered into her ear.

"I'm sure it does," Corrine answered. "How bout we save that for a little later."

"I so much want it now," Chet said as he began to kiss her neck.

"As much as I want to feel you in me, you know someone is going to come by with a question, concern or comment."

Chet eased off, then sat up and ruffled his hair. He glanced back towards their tent. "You're probably right… and low and behold."

Amy smiled as she and Jack approached, Amy sauntering in a playfully suspicious manner, her arms swinging casually across her body. She knew they had interrupted something. "Well just so you know, I'd be into swinging, but Jack here is more traditional."

Chet shot her a quizzical look. "That's what you came to inform me."

Jack took his hands out of his face but still shook his head in embarrassed disbelief. "No. Supper's ready, and we're all gathering to discuss our situation. Some are too exhausted to do anything, but we need to review a revised agenda before anyone hits the sack."

"Sounds like a good approach," Chet said. "We'll be right there."

The flames of the two fires dwindled as the night wore on. Only five people remained awake. Chet looked at his watch, 9:25 pm. "That hike really kicked some ass," he said looking at the remaining faces in the firelight. "I say we let the smaller fire burn out and concentrate on the larger one."

"I agree," Jack said fighting off a yawn. "Now about calls, should we do some or do you think it would cause a stir among the more tired?"

"I think starting off with some wood knocks would be a way to go," Chet said referring to the act of taking a heavy branch, bat or some kind of solid piece of wood and whacking it against a tree or another wood object.

"We came on the trip to research," Amy said holding a video recorder. "If the lambs need their rest, let them have it, but if I wanted to go camping, I would have done it somewhere else with a whole hell of a lot less walking. I say we do calls. We're here."

Chet laughed. He liked her spunk. She wore her 'don't give a shit' attitude well. It worked for her as a Goth girl dressed in black with her piercings all in place, but now, with her hair pulled back under a baseball cap, no piercings, and regular outdoor khaki clothes on, she resembled a plain Jane, girl next door type.

"I agree," Jack said. "We have two more nights after this, so let's get in as much as we can. No one said we couldn't do calls without another group."

"I'm in," Pacer and Sam said near simultaneously.

"Jack's gotta special wood knocking bat as well as two wood pieces to smack against each other," Amy said, amped that they were going to see if they could generate any kind of responses.

"Yes I do," Jack said as he stood up and went to their tent to retrieve the items.

"So… wood knocks on a tree or Jack's wood blocks?" Pacer asked glancing towards Chet.

Chet's mind drifted. Here they were, close to the scene where it all changed for him. In that flash of a moment he wondered what the hell he was doing, why was he back here? Images of those beasts ripped through his mind. He felt himself perspire. He also knew he had to snap back to real time before his mind sucked him into a cavernous nightmare of memories that would only terrify the rest of the group. "Well, I never used wood blocks, we just smacked a tree as it seemed more natural," Chet said hoping no one noticed he'd blanked out.

"Then let's start with that," Sam added. "Are you getting this on video?" he said to Amy who had been recording on and off since they pitched camp. Sam's cameraman had fallen dead asleep just after the sun set, having already shot lots of footage.

"Sure," she said with a smile. "Be glad to."

The five moved towards the edge of the camp where the light from the fire extended enough that they didn't need to use headlamps or flashlights. Jack and Chet found a tree that someone could wrap their arms around. Jack gripped his wood-knock-bat, a thirty-seven ounce wooden baseball bat that he taped thick around the handle with gaffer's tape. He thought it helped for better swinging against a solid object like a tree.

"Ready?" he asked.

"It's all you Jack," Chet said.

Jack swung the bat back then brought it through with a strong swing. *Dunnnk.* The sound was thick but not overly loud. They all stood silent waiting as the dim echo of the knock faded. Nothing.

"Do it again," Amy said, repositioning herself so the firelight shined on the scene more, giving her better footage.

Jack nodded, wound up his swing and hit the tree again but with a little more force. Again, nothing.

"Another," Sam said.

Jack repeated the hit. Nothing, no return knocks or calls.

"Try the wood blocks," Pacer said. "We've had pretty good luck with them in the past."

Sam handed the two smaller homemade bats to Jack. Holding them, the wood blocks resembled something like nightsticks that 19th-century English law enforcement carried with them while on patrol.

"Whenever you're ready," Chet said seeing Jack's anticipation.

Jack spread out his arms to full extension then swung the clubs into each other so they collided into an X. The crash of wood produced a higher pitch than that of the bat against the tree. It also echoed more, and all of them looked surprised by the amount of sound it produced. Again, they waited... nothing. Jack repeated smacking the two smaller bats. Again, nothing answered.

For almost an hour, they all took turns with different approaches to the knocks, but the same result occurred, nothing. It was after ten-thirty, and all five could feel the weight of the day begin to catch up.

"I don't know about you guys, but I'm going to guess there's nothing out there tonight," Sam said.

"I thought for sure we'd hear something," Amy said turning off the camera and feeling dejected.

"Don't worry, they know we're here," Chet said with confidence. He saw all the heavy eyes stare at him. "Believe me, we're not alone. They may not be close, but they aren't far."

"How do you know that?" Pacer asked.

"Because I know," Chet said not sure why he knew but just did.

"That's not really proof," Amy said.

"On this trust me, they're close enough," Chet said. "Let's get some sleep. I don't think we have anything to concern ourselves with tonight."

"If it's all the same to you, I'll keep a watch for a while," Pacer said.

No one objected.

Chet entered his tent. Corrine had left a small battery powered yellow night light on so he wouldn't have to fumble in the dark. He took off his shoes, jacket and one of his shirts before slipping out of his pants and getting into the sleeping bag.

"No success," he heard Corrine whisper.

"Nothing," he said, pleasantly surprised to find her awake. "Did you hear the knocks?"

"Some," she said, opening her eyes wider.

"Sorry if we woke you," Chet said bringing his face closer to her so he could kiss her.

"I actually tried to stay awake," Corrine said.

"Why?" Chet asked.

"I was hoping to get some of my own wood while out in the forest," she said with a grin, planting a deep open mouth kiss on Chet and pulling him on top of her.

"My favorite kind of knocking," Chet answered, returning the deep kiss, wrapping his arms around her so their bodies melded together.

Chapter 17

Chet rose early. He nearly always did. Aside from a few times after his release from prison, he rarely needed more than about five hours sleep a night. He stepped out of his tent to see the early wisps of the new day's light. Glancing around, he could see clearly the shapes of tents scattered about the edges of the clearing but not every defining detail. Peering into the woods, he could see a few yards in, but the darkness still clung to its depths. He moved a few steps away from his tent and onto one of the larger rocks that protruded from the ground. He noticed a body crouched over on the other side of the slope. He took a few steps to get a better look and noticed it was Bill.

"Morning," Chet whispered as he approached. "Find anything?"

Bill turned, his face filled with a wide-eyed, stunned expression.

"What?" Chet said, hurrying towards him. When he came next to Bill, he noticed what had caught Bill's eye.

"I thought I heard something last night, some rustling but I was so tired I didn't give it much mind," Bill said, his words slow and deliberate. "At first, I thought maybe I was dreaming."

"What exactly did you think you heard?" Chet asked, now kneeling down next to his long-time friend.

"I don't know," Bill said. "Like people walking by or something like that."

"You heard multiple footsteps?"

Bill took a moment. "Maybe, I don't know. Like I said, I thought I was dreaming."

"When did you find this?" Chet asked as he examined the remarkable impression in the ground.

"About a minute after I left the tent to pee. Not even ten minutes ago," Bill said. "That's one big ass footprint."

They both stared at a clearly defined footprint in the soft soil less than ten feet from Bill's tent and just into the tree line of the woods surrounding the clearing. The foot measured twenty-three inches long. The depression almost a third of an inch deep.

"Find any other tracks?" Chet asked.

"Actually I've just stared at this one. I haven't looked anywhere else," Bill said in his continued daze.

Chet felt a rush of warmth wash over him. He knew he was right about the creatures being around. "Let's have ourselves a little look-see and see if we can find any other presents embedded into the ground." He stood up, looked slowly around the immediate grounds, and then started to walk into the woods. He hadn't taken a couple steps when he signaled for Bill to come to him.

"Holy Shit," Bill said, staring down at another full footprint and a partial print almost right next to it. "We've got to make casts of this."

Chet nodded. "Indeed. You brought stuff, right?"

"Absolutely. So did Sam and Jack," Bill said with glee. "Let me get mine right now. See if you can spot anything else."

Chet moved about the immediate area with deliberate steps, careful not to accidentally smudge a potential print. He believed he found the general direction the creature exited the camp based on the three prints. With little effort, he spotted several other smaller depressions. Moving further from the perimeter and deeper into the woods, he spotted yet another print. He placed his foot next to it. Compared to his size twelve boot, his shoe looked like a child's next to it.

"That's one big ass Squatch."

Once news of the footprints broke to a few, the rest of the camp awoke almost instantaneously, abuzz with excitement. People swirled, and hovered around the found prints while others combed the surrounding woods hoping to discover their own find. Some folks suggested this become a base camp since it already revealed signs of activity. Jack wasn't sure. The worry became that the radios would not transmit over a mile, let alone two or three through the cluttered terrain. He didn't want a camp cut off from contact in case of an emergency.

Bill suggested that he and four others stay behind so they could fully investigate the surrounding area for more prints or any other signs of a presence. He also suggested that as long as they could keep radio contact, they should keep this location as one of the three camps. After all, he reminded them, their walkie-talkies had supposedly over ten miles of coverage.

Jack felt uncomfortable going off script this much, but Sam and Chet thought Bill's proposition a viable one. Jack acquiesced but only as long as they stayed in radio range. With that issue settled, the others broke down camp and began preparing to head out, leaving Nathan Avent, one of Bill's former grad students, Jeff Cass, a relatively new researcher, and two more veteran participants, Avery and Zachary to help out Bill.

Pacer and Jack worked the compass and topo map to determine the direction they needed to head towards. With little hesitation, they figured out which way to go and gave the signal to move out.

The woods closed in around the exiting group as they filed into a mostly single line. Chet and Corrine followed behind Pacer, Pete, Sam, Jack, and Amy. Harlan took the rear, a rifle slung over his shoulder in case of bear or worse. The rest filled the gaps in between.

The terrain, which started level, began to ascend five minutes into their walk. Soon they all found themselves breathing heavy at the ever-steepening slope.

"How much longer," a voice from the rear shouted after walking for nearly a half hour.

Jack turned, halted. "There's a dip in the terrain just ahead. We go through that, up a little bit more and the base camp will be there. Another ten or fifteen minutes."

The explanation puzzled Chet. He didn't remember seeing or experiencing any dips in the landscape when he had visited the area. All he could recall was a terrain that went up.

For another five minutes, they continued in a comfortable upward direction when an apparent ridgeline appeared. Chet watched as Pacer and Jack stopped at the top of the ascent, soon followed by Amy, Sam, and Pete. He and Corrine had fallen behind by about fifty feet. Most of the line had lengthened considerably on the walk. However, Chet noticed something different. The front five remained frozen in place. Their heads didn't turn. Their bodies didn't move. Chet felt Corrine's hand tighten around his.

"It's okay," he whispered as they came up the rise. "What's everyone looking at?" he asked, hoping to break the tense mood.

All five said nothing.

Chet's steps instantly became more cautious. His eyes darted back and forth in a frantic continuous scan. It reminded him of the prison yard when guys stayed on the lookout if they thought someone might knife them.

Coming to the top of the ridgeline, he froze. Unfolding before all of them, rows of mostly Douglas Firs pushed over in a tight rippling formation, leaning into and between standing trees. The pattern rolled out looking something like a giant wet paper Chinese fan draped over dowels on a rack. Looking more closely, Chet noticed the bottom of many of the trees were stripped almost clean of their root system.

"These things were transported here," he mumbled to himself in awe.

Looking beyond the giant tree structure, he noticed several single trees bent into arcs, looking like primitive catapults. The whole area of the dip in the landscape spanned close to two hundred feet.

"Holy shit," Corrine said, the words dropping out of her mouth as quick as her jaw hitting the floor. "What the hell is it?"

Chet didn't have a comprehensive answer.

"The Mecca of Sasquatch," Sam groaned with excitement. He turned to his cameraman. "Get that. All of it."

Pete took to his duties before Sam could even ask. He pulled out his small, high-end Canon XA10 camcorder. Weighing roughly two pounds, it produced a solid picture for a smallish camera. It was great for bushwhacking type trips. Pete powered it on, did a quick tech check of the settings and began to shoot the scene. He knew how Sam and the editing team liked footage shot. He started with doing several pans, then steady shots at fifteen-second clips, followed by several zoom ins and outs, both slow and fast. He also performed a couple herky-jerky style shots for good measure.

"You can tell this place is still used," Jack said aloud for anyone to hear.

Chet noticed. "The trees seem to all have a different wear and tear to them, showing that they are replaced as needed. You can see some of the trees in that large lean-to structure are more worn than others." He also pointed out a variety of dead trees lying on the ground, grown over by moss, ferns, and lichen.

The expedition team stood along the crest of the landscape stunned. Harlan, the designated group photographer, started to snap away. Those with phones soon started to do their own video and photo taking.

"What do you think the purpose of this place is?" Corrine asked to whoever might hear her question.

Chet shook his head. "Bill may know."

"Know what?" Sam asked. "Primates don't do this. I'm no expert, but I have done some studying on primates. At best, they may bend some branches or make an area on the ground more comfortable for themselves but nothing like this. This is beyond primate."

Chet listened. It was a hard assessment, but he knew Sam wasn't wrong.

"In fact, it may even be an insult to put these creatures into that category," Sam added.

"Then what category?" Jack asked, hearing the conversation and wanting to add his own two cents.

Sam didn't have an immediate answer as he continued to bathe his senses with the structures before him. "It's beyond any theory we can grapple with at the moment." Sam looked at both Chet and Jack hoping for more than stunned silence. "Come on guys... you've been through the myriad of possibilities for Sasquatch: Great apes, extinct apes, hybrid wild man, Neanderthals, aliens. I'm telling you... it's something more."

Jack smiled. "More than aliens?"

Sam bowed his head. "Shut up. You know what I'm driving at... something that we've never found in the fossil record. We keep wanting to tie Bigfoot to some kind of mammal, to give it a chain of evolution, a label to help us all sleep better. We like that– it makes things easier for the mind, it helps us picture a progression just like all those evolution of man posters. I think with this find, we are onto something entirely different concerning what we call Sasquatch. This is something with more than a primal or primate-like intelligence. What we have here is totally unique."

"That's kind of bold," Amy interjected.

"I don't think so," Sam replied. "It's just not the well-trodden path that everyone else likes to venture down. I'll be interested to see what Bill has to say about this."

"You know what guys?" Amy said. "I think it's time we take this show a bit closer and see what else we can discover about these structures."

"Absolutely," Sam chimed in. "Pete, you got this?"

A giant smile stretched across the cameraman's face like he just captured a Pulitzer prize winning shot. "You bet I do."

"We're going down there?" Corrine asked, squeezing Chet's hand.

"Hell yeah," Jack said. "We didn't come here for the camping, right?"

The rest of the expedition watched like kids witnessing a dangerous dare as Amy and Jack, followed by Chet and Corrine, made their way down the small slope and into the little valley. It wasn't until Chet and Corrine were in the confines of the giant tree structures that the others followed, first Sam, followed by Pete who recorded the others walking down towards the structures, then Pacer and the rest.

"Kind of looks like something out of Tolkien," Harlan said aloud.

"Not the part where the orcs tear down all the trees, I hope," Pacer shot back. Nervous laughter cluttered the air but quickly dissipated back to nothing more than the sounds of feet trampling on the forest floor.

"Careful!" Jack shouted while stopping abruptly.

"What?" Sam asked.

"Tracks," Jack said. "Look for tracks, footprints. Careful where you walk."

Nearly everyone's head shot towards the ground and began intensely searching. Even Chet gave a quick glance before turning his attention back to the towering structure and the bent over trees.

"Not to be funny but some of these arcs look like giant catapults," Corrine said keeping a safe distance from them.

"They do, but you can see how the tops are wedged into the lower branches of trees or held down by dead ones," Chet replied, appreciating the observation. "Some of the leaning trees in that fan resemble a step progression," Chet said as he moved closer to the large structure that dominated the landscape.

Corrine turned her attention away from the single trees and followed Chet's sight line to the larger structure. "And you can see how some of those tree tops, there's like twelve of them in that one spot, are really crammed into those wedges in the upper branches." She let out an exhale of impressed bewilderment.

"Are you okay?" Chet asked.

"I'm fine," she said as she grabbed his hand while continuing to stare up in awe. "How bout you?"

"I'm rather stunned, to be honest," Chet said as he too continued eyeing the magnificent assembly of trees and large branches. "If Jack is right about where my original camp really is, then we essentially pitched it right around the corner from this."

"You think they're out there now?" Corrine asked, her voice revealing a quiver.

Chet checked to see the proximity of people to them. He touched her cheek with a light stroke. "I think they've been watching us since we stepped ashore. At the very least, when we made our first camp."

"Nervous?" she asked, her eyes widening, hoping for some comforting words.

Chet swallowed hard. "I'd be lying if I said I wasn't."

"The others don't seem nervous," Corrine said as she turned to watch members of the group look for tracks and any other signs they could tie to Sasquatch.

"The others have no idea about these things. To them, it's still a fantasy," Chet said as he too observed the movements of the expedition.

The group didn't find footprints or signs that any Sasquatch had visited the locale in the recent past. Harlan took roughly three hundred pictures, all the while, marveling and wondering how any skeptic could say that the large fan like edifice surrounding them was man-made or a natural occurrence. He made sure to take wide, medium and close-up shots of the entire structure. He also recorded how some of the trees had the roots torn off, as well as a series of images that concentrated on the grounds so a skeptic couldn't claim the trees had fallen over in some way. As everyone witnessed, the grounds integrity, outside of a couple trees that were clearly pushed over and uprooted, never appeared compromised. The expedition crew began to call the find, Squatchtopia.

Jack looked at his watch and noticed they had roamed the site for over an hour. They were now several hours behind schedule after breaking camp late. He called for everyone's attention and informed them that they needed to move out. According to his estimation, they needed to walk another ten or fifteen minutes before they made it to their base camp. He said that once the base camps became settled, they could always come back to continue examining and recording the site.

As each of the crew crested the far ridge exiting the site, they all took one more glimpse at the magnificent craftsmanship they all believed a group of Bigfoot assembled. The layered fan shape, or as others deemed it, leant-to formation, stood like an ancient monolith, mesmerizing and daunting, stirring more questions than providing answers.

Within seconds of walking deeper into the woods, the expedition found themselves surrounded once again by tall trees and deafening quiet.

The terrain rose steadily but not steep. The greater obstacle became the undergrowth; ferns and layers of thick moss caked the forest floor, making it uneven, slippery and hard to keep solid footing. Fatigue began to rear its ugly head as breathing became labored and groans from muscle strain sounded off up and down the line of participants. A few had kept a close eye on their watches. Once the fifteen-minute mark came and went, they began to vocalize their displeasure.

Chet too began to wonder. Not that he wanted to complain, but the hike did seem to take longer than advertised and it grew later in the day making him question whether people would want to embark ever further into the woods to set up other camps. He also wondered about Bill, and whether a crew could return and retrieve him if needed. As far as he knew, only one radio transmission occurred just after they left the Squatchtopia site, and Bill answered it.

It took another fifteen minutes before Jack gave a shout that he and Pacer spotted the clearing. A roar of excitement and relief went up. Some began to worry they were lost. Chet thought if they had gone on for another couple minutes, a panic might have broken out among the group.

However, relief and joy erupted as the expedition entered the open space. The clearing was wider than the previous nights. The protruding stones were also smoother and less disruptive to the environment, making them easy to walk over, except one that rose up noticeably higher than the others. However, since there were no gaps between rocks large enough where someone could pitch a tent, everyone had to make camp around the periphery of the opening.

Chet reviewed the area. Nothing resonated. He thought for sure, images and feelings of what had taken place over a dozen years earlier would come flooding back, but the opposite happened, nothing felt right. In fact, he doubted this was the location Jack intended for the base camp.

"This is where you found the footage?" he asked Jack in a hushed tone not wanting to bring attention to the others.

Jack gave a quick account of the area and spotted the downed tree along the edge of the clearing where he had retrieved the camera. He guided Chet over to it. Pacer picked up on what was happening and met them at the moss-covered remains of the old fallen tree.

"This is the spot," Jack said pointing to the split in the trees trunk and the mostly hollowed out remains filled with small forest debris.

Pacer concurred, pulling out his phone and retrieving a picture of the site to double check.

Chet glanced at the photo. It was hard to tell. All the clearings looked similar. "Where then is my old base camp in relation to this one?" Chet asked. "Because this place doesn't look familiar to me."

"If Bill's team had joined us, either them or one of us would have gone over to it. It's only about a ten to fifteen minute hike from here in a northeasterly direction," Jack said. "You want to head over there?"

Chet didn't immediately answer, pondering whether he really wanted to revisit that spot. A sharp chill shuddered through him making his shoulders collapse forward in a quick jerk. "Not now. Maybe tomorrow." Something inside, like a primal voice from within his psyche, pushed at him, *Stay away*.

Just like the day before, when the expedition reached the previous camp, most just dropped their packs and wanted to take a couple minutes to catch some air. Jack didn't want Pacer's group to become too accustomed to their surroundings and urged the group that they should get moving quickly. Of the two sites to pick from, Pacer chose the location that had the easiest walk to it.

After a brief water break, Pacer and Harlan set out with the rest of their team. Chet and Corrine watched the group fade away into the thick of the woods almost moments after they embarked on it.

"How long should it take them to get to their camp?" Corrine asked, her eyes squinting in an effort to see their movement.

"It's not far, half a mile. In these woods, fifteen minutes if they keep a good pace," Chet answered.

"How far did we come from the previous camp?"

"Two-ish," Chet said. "It seemed longer because of the up and down of the landscape and our spending time at the structures. Radio contact with them should be easy. If we can talk to Bill's group, Harlan's group should have no problem keeping in touch with us," Chet said. "You okay?" he asked, now staring straight into her eyes.

"I'm fine," she answered sheepishly. "Just trying to get my bearings."

"You sure?" Chet said seeing how feeble she answered him. He reached out and put his finger under her chin to indicate he wanted her to look at him.

"Just an odd feeling," she said with a shrug.

"Scared? Concerned?" Chet asked.

"I guess… I don't know," Corrine said having stopped looking for the group in the woods. "I'm not afraid in the sense that I'm shaking, and my mind is unraveling. I guess I'm more numb to it all, not sure what to think. Tell you what, let's get some firewood and talk about something different."

Chet smiled. "Sounds good."

The late day air turned chillier. Sweaters and jackets became a necessity. The site's fire roared warmer and bigger than the previous two night's fires. Frequent radio checks revealed all the camps had settled in. Bill's group found one other footprint and made a cast of it. Pacer's group reported nothing out of sorts. They had a fire going and were waiting for the onset of night.

Eleven o'clock took a long time to arrive. Anticipation for getting the investigation under way gripped them all like children waiting to open up Christmas presents.

Headlamp lights bounced around the clearing as folks prepared for their roles in the upcoming evening's research. On the night's agenda, different people would be performing howls, recording audio, video, spotting with the thermals, making wood knocks and taking notes. Each member had his or her specified role, but everyone would have a chance at a howl or whoop if they wanted to perform one.

Corrine volunteered to take notes much to the relief of everyone in their group, including Amy who generally did that task. Most looked at that assignment as tedious, if not difficult because of the preciseness needed.

Amy and Pete manned the audio and video gear. Both had started to collect a lot of footage, especially with the discovery of Squatchtopia. Pete videoed Sam doing a few 'talk to's' into the camera, much like one sees on reality shows. No one asked Chet any questions or to participate, but both Peter and Amy stole a few shots of him walking, talking and checking out the setup of camp as well as him examining the squatch structures.

Sam and Jack agreed to alternate the night vision gear. They also agreed to split radio duties. No one asked Chet to take a specific role, but he volunteered for knocks, radio, and thermal detection duty, whatever role needed tending.

"It's just after eleven," Jack said to Sam who stood nearby going over the thermal camera using the red light on his headlamp to look at the controls. Every member of the expedition had red lights on their headlamps. Red light kept the pupils from closing, which would make it harder to see in the dark. "I think it's time for a radio check."

"Let's get this rolling at 11:20 and we'll alternate camps every twenty minutes," Sam said, confirming their agenda.

Jack took out his radio and called the two camps. "Twenty minutes to first attempts. Everyone should have their duties square and gear running by then. We'll start, Camp 1 at 11:20, then Pacer's, Camp 2 at 11:40 and Bill, Camp 3 at the midnight. All calls and knocks will happen after a ten count. We'll mix and match calls from all the camps after the midnight sounding."

Both camps checked Jack's message. "Lead the way," Pacer shot back.

Chet stared at his watch, eyeing every second counting off on his green glowing digital output.

"You ready for this baby?" Corrine asked; pad in hand with pen and her headlamp's red light on. She had noticed Chet's quieter demeanor as the evening progressed.

"I'm fine," he answered.

"It's okay if you're a little tense honey," Corrine said before leaning her head on his shoulder for a moment.

He kissed her. "Thank you. I'm all right. Just weird to be back here after all this time."

Chet headed towards Jack and Sam who congregated near the fire by Amy. She held a high-end consumer video camera that allowed for interchangeable lenses. Jack had purchased it a couple months before the expedition along with a 1.4 aperture lens knowing it was his best bet for capturing footage in low light.

"Let's get ready to do this," Sam said, a broad smile widening across his face as he brought the radio up to his mouth. "Camp2, Camp3, this is Camp 1 you copy."

"Roger that," both camps shot back almost stepping on top of each other.

"Ready for a howl from Camp 1. Jack will get the night's proceedings going in ten," Sam said.

All of them began a soft-spoken ten count. At the count of one, Jack dipped his chin into his neck having taken a deep breath, brought his hands to his mouth like a megaphone and let rip a long steady howl. The sound echoed around Camp 1, floating in the air for a few moments before fading away. They all stood silent, waiting. They heard nothing in return. Sam waited a few more seconds before calling out over the radio again.

"Camp 1 howl complete… anyone hear a return?"

"Negative," came the responses.

"Try again," Bill said, his radio transmission crackling with static.

"Check," Sam answered. "Getting ready for another howl in ten."

Again, Jack let out a loud and long howl, letting his voice trail off more this time. The howl hung in the air before falling away. They waited but heard nothing in return.

"Could faintly hear yours this time but no responses," Pacer said.

"Nothing," Bill added.

"Roger that Camp 2 and 3," Sam said. "We're going to try a few wood knocks. If nothing, then we'll wait for the next interval. Report if you hear anything."

"Roger that," they answered.

Chet took the wood knock clubs Jack had fashioned and gave them three successive but slow whacks. Again, they stood waiting, but nothing happened.

"I guess we'll wait and see if anything turns up later," Sam said. "For now, we might as well enjoy the fire."

The 11:40 and midnight calls made by the other camps garnered no responses. Eerie silence followed their echoing calls. As the evening wore on, the darkness felt as if it closed in on all of them like a shrinking box. Chet had to remind the camps, as did Jack, Sam, and Pacer, that the night was still young, that in fact, most Sasquatch activity didn't begin to pick up until after two in the morning in their experiences.

At 3:30, eyes grew heavy. Whispers of calling off the night at 4 am permeated through all the camps. Nothing, not even an owl or wolf answered their calls or knocks. Chet would not let the lack of success dampen their efforts. He slapped backs, thighs, shook shoulders and even sprinkled in a few prison stories to keep his group alert. He didn't often like talking about his time in jail but knew the topic would perk ears and help keep people awake.

"Come on," Chet said, clapping his hands as he stood up and circled the camp. "Let's get this going again, only a few more rounds, then a big breakfast and we can crash."

The others in the camp moved slower, but all of them got up.

"How about starting off with a whoop call," Chet said to Sam seeing he had the most trouble staying awake. "A couple of those will keep the blood flowing."

Sam nodded, standing half-asleep. "Okay, give me a moment."

Chet took the radio and called the other camps attention. It took a minute for both to respond before Chet informed them of what was to take place. "The TV star here is going to give out an inspired whoop in ten," Chet said, full of more energy than anyone really wanted to hear.

Sam stood erect, shook off his doldrums, took a deep breath, brought his cupped hands to his mouth and gave out a powerful whoop, followed by another, then a third less powerful one. They all stood and waited. Silence again answered them and the other camps.

"One more time," Chet said, then reported into the radio that Sam would give it another shot.

As soon as the camps acknowledged another attempt, a distant, faint call streamed through the silence. Smiles and wonderment adorned the faces of those in Chet's camp. Everyone admitted to hearing what sounded like a howl.

"Response heard," Pacer reported, his voice excited."

"Roger that," Chet said. "Bill, how about you guys, anything?"

"Negative, we didn't hear anything," Bill shot back.

"Copy that," Chet answered. "We'll respond with a howl in ten." Chet looked at Sam. "You're the man with the golden tonsils, give it another go."

Sam nodded, took in a deep breath and let out another long deep howl.

The group waited in silence. Again, a call answered, a distant wail with a touch of a bass feel to it, but one thing about it stood out - it was closer than the previous call.

"Heard that!" Bill shouted through the radio.

"Roger that," Chet said. Before he could ask, Pacer responded that they had heard it as well, and louder.

"I think they must be closer to you Pacer," Chet said. "Bill's camp heard nothing the first time - heard it this time, we heard it too, and it was louder."

"Roger that," Pacer shot back. "Definitely louder. If it's a squatch, then it's to our eastern direction."

"Why don't one of you guys give it try," Chet said to Pacer.

"Roger," Pacer responded. The radio went silent for a moment. "Harlan will give a whoop in ten."

About ten seconds later Corrine and Jack signaled to the others that they heard the whoop, though faint they could make it out. However, this time, instead of waiting seconds for a response, one came immediately. Short whoops with a few clicks broke the silence of the night.

"Did you catch that Bill?" Chet asked.

"Negative, we didn't hear anything," he answered.

Chet expressed his puzzlement. The sound came back stronger and more distinct. He couldn't understand why they didn't hear it.

"Duration," Corrine said. "The other calls had longer durations, these were shorter calls. Maybe the sound just didn't travel as well."

"Good thought," Chet answered. "Have Harlan try a howl rather than a whoop, Bill's camp heard nothing, wondering if a howl resonates better in the air than a whoop."

"Roger that," Pacer replied. "A howl in ten."

Camp 1 heard Harlan's call as faint as it was. Bill's did not. They all waited for a response. Nothing. They waited another minute, nothing.

"Maybe that's it," Pacer radioed.

"We'll give it a shot here and see what happens," Chet said. He turned to Corrine. "Why don't you give a call a try?"

Corrine reacted with surprise. She had practiced a couple howls and whoops but didn't think it would ever fall to her to do one, nor did she care if she ever did. The camps all had enough eager participants to give them. "Why me?"

"Because you can," Amy said, placing her hand on Corrine's shoulder giving it a shake. "Give it a go girl, come on."

Corrine appreciated the support but still felt wary.

"You can do it, baby," Chet said giving a reassuring nod.

"Maybe the worry in your call will spark something," Jack said.

"I'm not worried," Corrine shot back not liking the accusation.

"Good," Jack said with a nod. "Then you won't have a problem doing one."

Corrine read what he was trying to do, and it worked. She brought her hands up to her mouth open cup style and gave a loud bellowing yell. The yell had hints of a scream of terror to it that echoed around them louder than the previous calls.

"Wow," Chet whispered. Amy echoed the sentiment.

A few seconds passed then a long deep, reverberating guttural return call sounded. Where the other calls floated through the air, distant and harmless, this one cut the silence of the night like a deep pounding drum. The sound roared through the air with a heaviness none of the others had. And, it sounded closer than any of the previous responses.

"Shit," did you hear that?" Sam asked, his eyes wide with surprise. "I never heard anything like that before. Did we get that on video or audio?"

"Sure did," Peter said, his eye fixed in the viewfinder of the camera pointing at the group. "I saw the audio bars move. It's on file."

A chill shot through Chet's body. "I've heard that before." He turned to Corrine. She stood frozen.

"I've heard that call too," she said.

"Holy shit," a voice crackled over the radio. It was Bill. "That call rolled through here with chilling gusto. We're still shaking. It was as if we could feel it."

"Roger that," Chet answered still staring at Corrine whose shoulders began to relax, but her face remained stoic. "Pacer, you hear that?"

"Hear it? Christ, I nearly shit myself," he answered. "Never heard anything like that before."

"I have," Chet said. "That's a Sasquatch."

"Tell you what... it's getting closer," Pacer shot back.

"Yes, it is," Chet said, handing the radio to Jack.

"What are you doing?" Jack asked.

"Getting my shotgun," Chet said.

Jack didn't like Chet's answer. "Is that necessary?"

"Hopefully not," Chet said emerging quickly from his tent, weapon in hand. "But if you think I'm being caught off guard... you're nuts. This is exactly the reason why I insisted on at least two rifles a camp. You hope you don't ever have to use it, and you don't ever want to say, I wish I brought a gun." Chet then pumped the shotgun, chambering a shell.

"You're making me nervous," Amy said.

"Easy guy," Sam said with his hands out bobbing slightly motioning for him to calm down.

"We're on alert," Chet said in all seriousness. "I don't mean to scare you, but it's time to consider the tragic 'what if' and I'm not going down without a fight if it comes to it."

Chet could see everyone's frozen expressions as if paused in time. "Sam," Chet said with authority. "Sling that rifle of yours over your shoulder."

Without hesitation, Sam retrieved his rifle.

The others instantly found themselves with a completely different appreciation and understanding for Chet's feelings. To them, he was a legendary investigator, something of a folk hero. Yet now, some began to look at him as crazed, maybe even mad. Amy nuzzled up closer to Jack, squeezed his bicep. Telepathically, she tried to tell Jack that she now believed Chet might have killed all those people and that those calls they just heard triggered some kind of psychosis.

"Hey man, relax a little," Jack said trying not to reveal his own nervousness. "That call was still ways off in the distance. Too far really."

"Really," Chet said with a smirk. "And they're getting closer by the moment."

"But," Jack said.

Chet cut him off. "You saw that tape. Did you think that was fiction? Get your head out of your ass. I'm not asking you to go to battle, but I want you all to be ready and alert. We're a long way from home folks, wake up," Chet said. In the ensuing silence, he could see their nervous expressions. He could feel their doubts about his innocence creep over them.

Chet relaxed his grip on the rifle. The tightness around his face loosened. Taking a depth breath, he slung the rifle back over his shoulder. Without waiting for any kind of response, he told Jack to continue a constant pan of the perimeter with the thermal device to see if anything was lurking about.

Chet took a couple of deep breaths. "Sorry for the fright. I'm telling you, those things don't fuck around. If they show up, it isn't so they can parade themselves in front of the camera." He paused, settling himself more. "And tell everyone else to get their thermal gear going if they haven't already."

"That I can do," responded Jack who then retrieved the equipment only a few feet away. Turning it on, he immediately began to walk around the edge of the clearing, dutifully scanning.

"Radio the other camps to have their rifles close by," Chet said more easily to Sam, who immediately responded to the request.

Another moment of silence ensued. Amy wanted to pivot the mood of the camp. "Should we do another call or are we canceling that idea?" she asked, her voice still shaking a bit.

"We continue forward, but prepared," Chet said. "Radio Bill's camp to do a howl, they haven't tried in a while. Also, remind them to have their weapons nearby."

Twenty seconds later, a very faint call emerged from the direction of Bill's location. It took another moment before several distant whoops responded. They weren't nearly as intimidating as the howl everyone heard earlier, but it was clear, more than one creature was returning the call.

"I think I have something," Jack shouted, waving his hand for someone to come over, not taking his eye off the screen.

Amy came first, followed by Chet. Sam, Pete, and Corrine stood back, looking and listening to their surroundings.

"It's off in the distance, the elevation goes up in this direction," Jack said pointing into the dark woods, in a southerly direction. "A small figure, but something on the screen moved."

"I saw it," Amy blurted. "Way off, barely registers. How far does this thing work?"

"Some devices can see up to five hundred yards or more," Jack answered. "I just have no sense of immediate depth with it."

"That one can see far out into open spaces, fifteen hundred yards," Sam added. "It has a medium length lens but a great sensor and resolution. In here, probably a lot less with all these trees and growth but it should still detect something pretty far out if the sight line is there."

"You sure you saw something, not just some play of the imagination?" Chet asked, retrieving the radio back from Sam.

"I definitely saw something," Amy said. "I'm sure of it."

"Keep an eye on it for another minute... if it doesn't move, keep working the area," Chet said. "Mark the spot and we can come back to it." He then asked for thermal reports from the other camps, but the news came back negative.

"Should we continue with the calls?" Amy asked.

"Maybe give it a rest for a couple minutes, see what comes of it," Sam suggested.

Chet nodded and relayed the information to the other camps, who all agreed with the plan.

Ten minutes passed. Jack saw nothing more on the thermal and neither did any of the other camps on their devices.

"We're going to give a howl," Bill reported, breaking the radio silence. "Any objections?"

Chet asked Jack and Sam for guidance, and they both gave a thumbs up. "Check, go when ready."

Doing ten counts in their heads, they then heard a very faint call float in the air, not loud enough to record on any device they had. Again, a moment passed before a distinct return whoop sounded, followed by several clicks and wood knocks.

"That's coming from the direction of the structures," Sam said, realizing the sound had a more direct track to it.

"I think he's right," Amy said, pointing towards where the sound came from in nearly the same direction they entered into their camp.

Corrine nodded that she agreed. Jack and Chet weren't sure.

Chet knew the only way to truly know was to ask. "Bill… was wondering if you could locate the direction of the call?"

"Roger that," Bill said, his voice tense. "Sounded like its coming from where you guys exited this camp to get to yours."

"Everything okay? You sound a little tight," Chet said.

"We're ready just in case. Jeff has a rifle at his side," Bill said, his voice containing the hints of a tremble. "And I have mine."

"Easy Bill… keep us posted if anything happens," Chet said. "Breathe easy."

"Will do," Bill returned.

Chapter 18

Chet looked at his watch, 4:10. He glanced up at the sky; the once cloudless night began to turn partly cloudy. He figured about another ninety minutes of darkness before the first glimpse of the new day would show itself. The excitement of calls recharged everyone but almost twenty minutes had gone by since the last sign of responses. Many times in the past, an active night would suddenly end without any rhyme or reason. Yet, he also knew that just because activity dwindled down, didn't mean activity ended.

"What was that?" Jack shouted as he jumped to his feet having almost fallen asleep while sitting with his back to the fading fire, looking out into the woods with the thermal in his lap.

"What?" Chet said, snapping out of his own oncoming daze.

"I thought I heard something hit the ground," Jack said.

"I don't understand," Amy said.

Then they all heard it, a thump, followed by something rolling along the ground. Each of them thought the sound came from a different direction, so all their heads turned in complete disorder.

"Something is throwing stones at us," Chet said, as he went low to the ground and swung his shotgun out in front of him. "Jack, start panning that thermal and see if you can spot something."

Another object came out of the air, this time hitting the rocky surface a few feet from where they sat. The clack and skip of the rock had them all crouch into defensive stances, like that of a cornered animal.

"Camps one and two, we have activity," Chet blurted into his radio as he peered into the darkness of the woods.

"Something is throwing stones at us."

"Copy that," Pacer answered. "We thought we heard footsteps in the woods a short time ago but saw nothing on the thermal."

Another stone then another came crashing down, skipping a few feet away from Sam and Pete. "We just had more come our way, closer this time," Chet said.

"Anything we can do?" Pacer asked.

"Negative," hold your ground," Chet said. "Jack, did you get that damn thermal going?"

Jack had to turn it on, which he fumbled with in the dark. He positioned the device in the direction he believed the throws came from.

"Anything?" Corrine asked, her voice desperate.

"A minute, I just turned the fucking thing back on," Jack shot back, sweat flowing off his brow, onto his hands and some onto the device's screen.

Two more stones came crashing down at the same time, smacking against the open rock surfaces. Amy rushed closer to Jack, wrapping her arms around him.

"What the fuck is going on," Sam said as he tried to see who or what was throwing the rocks while bringing his rifle around.

"Are we under attack?" Amy asked, her voice now trembling.

"Not yet," Chet said, his voice strong and steady. "Stone throwing isn't unusual."

"I've never heard of anything like this," Sam said, his voice quivering trying to hold it together.

"Got something," Jack shouted.

Chet crawled over to Jack who was about fifteen feet away. "What?"

"Two beings… Look, look, look," Jack said his voice excited as they both watched a large form bend down, pick up an object and underhand hurl it in their direction, while a second figure stood motionless next to it, nearly fading into the framework of the forest.

This time, they heard the stone go through some trees before crashing down behind them far enough away that the stone harmlessly rolled into the woods.

"That's friggin' wild," Chet said gazing at the screen. "Look at the size of them."

"I have no real way to judge their height, but what, at least eight or nine feet tall," Jack said.

"What the hell are you guys doing?" Amy half shouted. "Get them to stop."

"They don't seem hostile," Jack said.

"They don't do they," Corrine snapped back, the sarcasm foaming. "Next time you throw a party, how about I start showering it with rocks and tell your guests it's merely harmless stone play."

"What I mean is…" Jack said before Amy cut him off.

"Think we give a shit about scientific research right now," Amy shot back, her breathing heavy and frantic. Another stone came hurtling by, crashing, a few rock splinters hitting them before rolling away. "It's not like we can run away to our cars and get out of here. We're being fucking attacked."

Chet didn't think this was an attack - more like a warning. He'd experienced something similar in Mount Baker-Snoqualmie National Park, Washington when he and a group of four others had rocks and small branches thrown at them for several minutes. Some of those members panicked too. His memory then flashed back to the attack that sent him away, the screams, the panic. *Those things tossed stones too before they…*

Chet shook his head to snap back to the moment at hand. "Still see them?" he asked.

"I do," Jack answered.

"What's going on?"

"They're standing. Just standing," Jack said. "Now they've backed away, standing behind trees or maybe they just faded out. Shit, I can't tell. Is the battery dying in this thing?"

"Shouldn't be. We put brand new ones in at the base camp," Sam shot back.

Off in the distance, several soft but completely audible whoops with tenor overtones sounded. All the members in the camp heard it.

"Look at that," Jack whispered so only Chet could hear.

"What?" Chet said, positioning himself so he could look at the screen.

"Well at first they stopped all movement then looked to walk out of the screen."

"Can you still see them?" Chet asked.

"Yes, but now they look to be standing out in the open," Jack said with puzzlement. "Like they're presenting themselves."

Chet managed to see enough. The creatures were distinct in the frame; their gray/white shapes standing against a dark background. However, after a few more seconds, the two creatures faded from view, as if absorbed into the environment.

"What the fuck?" Amy said.

"Shouldn't we see color?" Corrine asked, her hand on Chet's back.

"I inverted the imaging," Sam said. "Works better for this type of environment."

Several whoops broke through the night air.

Chet pulled the radio off his belt. "Who made the whoop? Did anyone make a call?"

"Negative," came the responses.

"Was waiting to give another call," Pacer said.

"Did you hear the whoops?" Chet asked.

"We heard it. It was clear and distinct. We recorded it as well," Bill interjected.

"Everything okay?" Chet asked not really knowing why.

"Yeah, we're fine… everything there okay? You sound a little frazzled," Bill said.

"Just a minor moment," Chet said. "We had an encounter of sorts."

The radio flooded with questions, each member stepping over the next making it so Chet couldn't hear any of the questions.

"Relax," Chet had to say a few times before the chatter died down. "We had a stone-throwing incident. And one even better – visual on the thermal."

"No way," Pacer shot back like an excited fifth grader. "How cool must have that been?"

"If he thinks shitting himself is cool, he can have it," Amy barked.

"It was a bit intense, to say the least," Chet said. "A little close for comfort."

"Did you record it?" Bill asked.

The air went out of all of them. In the excitement/panic of the moment, Jack forgot to record the readings. Pete had positioned himself about ten feet away from Sam and Chet, video recording the whole incident but he never filmed the screen.

"Negative," Chet said with both an air of remorse and anger.

"But I have audio and reactions to what just took place," Pete added.

"At least we have that," Sam added.

"No worries, we still have some time," Bill answered. "How bout if we send out a call and see what comes of it?"

"Take it away," Chet said.

"Okay then, will give a howl in ten."

Ten seconds later, a faint call wisped through the air. This time, though, no one had to wait as a series of calls and whoops sounded all around all the camps. Some seemed distant while others closer, all echoing, colliding and coalescing into one howl.

"Did we get that?" Chet asked.

"Yes," Amy said panning her camera around the camp, transfixed by the sound that hung in the air. She did all she could to steady her trembling hands.

"Me too," Pete added.

"That was frickin' wild," Sam said. "Like crowd noise in a stadium." Sam turned to Pete, told him to turn on the fill light mounted on his camera. "I'm going to do a quick spot. No way I'm letting this slip by. Ready… in five, four, three… It's after four a.m. Our camp has heard all kinds of howls and whoops. At times the sounds have surrounded us so we have no idea of an exact direction from where they are coming from. It's been bone chilling at times. Just a short time ago, we experienced stones being tossed at us then as fast as it started, it stopped. Quite frankly, I thought we were under attack, but the stones missed us by a safe distance. We suspect they may be just warning us about being in their territory. Still, very harrowing and fascinating at the same time. Without a doubt, this is the most prolific moment of my career. After hearing these calls, experiencing the stones being thrown at us, there is no doubt as far as I'm concerned and the others participating in this expedition that the creature we call Bigfoot, exists."

Before Sam could go on, another series of howls echoed around them, some distant, others near.

Sam's face lit up with excitement at having captured the moment and his reaction. "Can you hear that? Another round of calls. Wild beyond belief. We are in the thick of Bigfoot territory," he said looking straight into the camera.

A gap of silence filled the air.

"Are you done over there Hollywood?" Amy said, her lips curled into her mouth biting on her contempt for Sam's showmanship.

Sam rolled his eyes at her sarcasm. "Hey, this is real. This is serious but at the same time, you have to be able to sell it. Sorry if you aren't in line with my methods."

Another call cut through the air, this time, it was singular, baritone in nature and loud.

"Did you guys hear that?" Chet asked into his radio.

"Affirmative," came the responses.

Pacer then said his group was going to vocalize a howl. Ten seconds later, Chet and crew heard their faint call. It sounded louder than Bill's group but still distant. Again, they didn't have to wait long for a response. Almost immediately, howls and whoops filled the air, this time, louder, closer, too close for some.

"How many do you think made that sound?" Jack asked thinking he heard several.

Chet didn't have a real idea but gave his thoughts. "A dozen, maybe more."

"Me too," Sam said.

"A dozen?" Corrine said, her grip tightening around Chet's forearm. "What dozens? Don't tell me this is happening."

Chet could see Corrine's terror reemerge. Her once confident eyes glazed over to panic, helplessness. He needed her to hold steady. The middle of the woods, a whole day's journey away from civilization was no place for a meltdown. He needed her to get a grip; otherwise, she could possibly pose a danger to all of them.

Chet turned to her, locked eye contact. "Listen, daybreak is an hour away. It'll start getting light soon. You need to keep it together. You have the strength. I know you do. You know you do." He could see she needed some reassuring, not a scolding. "Do you understand what I'm saying?"

"Yes. Sorry."

"I knew you had the strength," Chet said seeing her relax a little. "You are strong. Keep strong."

"So what next?" Sam asked, interrupting the two of them. "Do we keep calling, see what happens?"

"I say no," Amy said, worried, her body shaking, sweat beginning to appear on her face as she tried to hold steady her camera. "No need to antagonize."

"I agree," Corrine said. "No need to become a beacon for these things."

"We're beyond that," Chet said. "They know we're here. What we do now has little consequence on what they will do."

"Are you saying we're fucked?" Amy snapped, not expecting that answer.

"I'm saying we're in their territory. We have to be alert," Chet said with more force. "That's why we have fucking rifles." Chet swung his shotgun around to his front. "And this is why it's loaded." Chet once again could see their astonished faces in the glimmer of red headlamp light as he looked at all of them. Taking a deep breath, he swung the rifle back over his shoulder.

"Or we could simply be making this out to be more than it is," Jack said, hoping to diffuse the tension.

"He's right," Amy added as if trying to convince herself. "Sound travels funny in the mountains. You say a dozen of them, but it may actually be a few but spread out. Echoes can sound larger than their source."

Chet felt they were wrong; knew they were wrong. He didn't want to make a case out of it. He knew they were deluding themselves to save their sanity and keep from panicking.

"Pacer," Chet said into his radio. "How are you guys doing?"

"We're okay," Pacer answered, his voice not conveying assuredness.

"Good. Tell you what. We could use your presence here. Any chance of that happening?" Chet asked.

"Let me check," Pacer answered.

"Everything okay buddy?" Bill asked.

"Yup," Chet said. "Just trying to tighten things up. How bout you?"

"We're good actually, weirded out a little, but confident," Bill said. "We have weapons. We're okay for now."

Chet smiled. "Good. Hold that fort."

"We're bugging out," Pacer answered with no hesitation. "Everyone agrees. It feels like it's getting hairy. No pun intended."

Another howl sounded followed by a whoop, then several more howls and wood knocks. Again, a wall of sound filled the air, none of it loud but all of it feeling near.

Chet looked up at the sky. Clouds blanketed the stars. Glancing at his watch, they had under an hour to sunrise, but little had changed in the lighting. It still felt like the middle of the night. "Come on sunrise, happen already," he mumbled to himself.

Another howl pierced the pocket of silence. This one like a shriek of terror, high pitched and closer.

"Hear that Bill," Chet asked, searching for the originating point of the call as he ducked to the ground.

"Hear it," Bill said, his voice sounding shrill, heightened with tension. "It sounded like two of them were right outside our camp."

"Get the thermal on them, record it," Chet half shouted back.

"Shit Chet… now I think I know exactly how you guys felt."

"You're good. Just keep it together, weapons ready if needed," Chet answered.

More howls sounded, some close some distant, layering on top of each other. Chet and company could feel a reverberation shudder through their bodies. Amy began to cry. Corrine came close to Chet, touched his sweater but otherwise kept calm and quiet.

"Let's keep close, near the fire," Chet directed. "Keep all the headlamps on normal, form a circle, this way we have all our angles covered. Jack, you still have the thermal on?"

"Absolutely. But so far, nothing."

"Keep that thing trained on the woods, keep scanning, let's see if we can figure out what we're up against. You stay red so you can read that thing," Chet said.

Corrine tugged at Chet. He turned to her. She forced a crooked smile, then whispered. "You think we're okay... I mean honestly?"

Chet paused. He had no idea. "We stick together. The other group gets here. We'll be fine. Strength in numbers, superior firepower."

She nodded but the gesture came off empty as if her fate resigned. "One last thing," Corrine said, then grabbed Chet's face and gave him a kiss. "I love you."

"Hey," Chet said with soft, compassionate romanticism as he placed three fingertips on her cheek. "We're okay. Everything is fine. We just can't let our imagination start running the show."

She cracked a nervous grin. "Yeah... that never has done anyone any good."

He turned her face directly to his. "I love you too."

Chapter 19

Pacer made sure his crew gathered all their basic essentials for getting out: weapons, light sources and recording devices. Pacer understood Chet's theory of larger numbers favored safety. He figured all decisions concerning the rest of the expedition would happen once the two camps merged.

A few more Sasquatch calls sounded, some close, most further off. However, he couldn't worry about calls for the moment. He had to make sure his crew made it back to Chet's camp safely.

"Everyone ready?" Pacer bellowed so the group could hear him. Affirmatives answered. Pacer had Alex follow close behind him with one of the rifles. The headlamps cut definitive swaths of light in the deep darkness of the woods as they exited the camp. Pacer proceeded slowly making sure the footing felt secure. It would take a couple minutes to get used to the soft flooring of the forest and for the crew to get into a comfortable night stride. Pacer estimated it would take a half hour before arriving at Chet's camp walking in the dark. But time wasn't his concern. What he worried about, was what they would do if they ran into a Bigfoot or worse, several of them? He initially second-guessed the idea of leaving the site, not sure it was wise given there was only another hour or two of true darkness before they could see well. However, the others all wanted out once he mentioned Chet's idea and he didn't feel like having a debate over it.

"Keep the line tight," Pacer heard Stan Bennett say from the rear. Stan had a rifle, as did Harlan who walked in the middle of the group.

Not five minutes passed into their journey through the blackened maze of trees when several more calls erupted all around them. In a layered succession, the calls started far away and slowly came closer. Pacer could feel his heart pound, and he began to walk with a faster stride.

"What the fuck is all that?" Stan shouted. Stan had the least experience with Sasquatch expeditions. The two prior ones he participated in resulted in no activity.

"Just keep pace and the line moving," Pacer said without losing any speed. He looked at his compass and saw he was on the right course. Most of the trip would be on level ground or a slight decline. Pacer knew if they kept a steady, slow to moderate pace, they should avoid any issues with balance and steadiness. The last thing they could afford was someone getting hurt.

"We just keep moving," Pacer said. "Stay the course." As he continued on, another wave of calls encircled them, no closer, no further away, just around them like an invisible shell. He tried his best to ignore the calls and just keep going. As he trudged on, he thought he heard a few whimpers of crying behind him.

"I've got something on the thermal," Harlan shouted from the middle of the line.

The pace slowed as everyone circled around Harlan.

"What, where?" Pacer asked.

"Straight that way," Harlan said pointing in a northerly direction.

"Can't see anything?" Pacer said adjusting his view to the screen.

"It was there... two of them... maybe a hundred or so feet in."

"Fine, keep an eye on it, otherwise, let's keep moving, standing here in the middle of nowhere doesn't serve us any good," Pacer said, before breaking from the huddle and double checking his compass.

Not ten steps into the continuation of the walk, something passed through the far reaches of Pacer's headlamp light. Like a deer on alert, he stopped dead in his tracks and stared straight out into the light.

"Something wrong?" Alex asked nearly barreling into Pacer.

"You didn't see anything?" Pacer asked, moving forward but at a more cautious pace.

"No," Alex said lifting the barrel of the rifle to waist level and searching the area more thoroughly. "What did you see?"

"Not sure. I thought something moved through the area up ahead."

"You think we would have heard it?" Alex asked.

"Makes sense," Pacer said. "Anything on the thermal?" he asked, his voice louder.

"Nothing," came back Harlan's reply.

Pacer breathed a little easier but couldn't shake the notion that he saw something. He began to pick up his speed again when this time something did move at the end of his headlamps' light. Alex saw it too. For a second, maybe two, a large, hairy creature from head to toe, stood squarely in the weak light. Brown with a dark face, its eyes glazed a hollow gray-green in the catch-light of Pacer's headlamp. It stood between eight and ten feet tall, broad-shouldered like a giant linebacker in football. Then as quick as it appeared, it melded back into the darkness of the forest. Pacer and Alex stopped. They couldn't move, and the group eventually caught up seeing their frozen bodies, petrified into place.

"What's going on?" Stan asked, bringing his rifle up to his side, his left hand securing the wooden stock.

"We saw something," Alex said.

"What?" Stan asked, squinting his eyes to see if he could see anything.

"The biggest Sasquatch ever," Pacer added.

"No shit," Harlan said, half excited, half frightened. "What did it look like?"

"Like every other realistic Bigfoot picture, except bigger," Pacer added. "It seemed to present itself to us."

"So now what?" Harlan asked as he continued to scour the scene with the thermal but sighting nothing, his hands beginning to shake.

"We keep moving, keep the line tighter and get to Chet's camp," Pacer said as he stepped forward and once again headed in the line they needed to travel.

"Why can't I see it?" Harlan asked, frustrated. "I mean, if you just saw it, it couldn't have gone too far and even if it did, this device has excellent range. I should be able to easily spot something within the range of your headlamp."

It was a good question. Pacer had no plausible explanation nor did he have the want or time to ponder it. He just wanted to get to Chet's camp.

"We can discuss the merits of it later. Right now, I just want to keep moving," Pacer shot back, the perspiration mounting as droplets poured down the side of his face. He continued forward and amped up the pace, his own nerves acting as a throttle.

After another hundred yards of walking, more screeches and calls rained down around them.

"How much further?" Alex asked softly to Pacer so no one else could hear his nervousness.

"Shouldn't be too far," Pacer said. "No more than another ten minutes."

The Sasquatch calls felt like they brushed up against the skin, sending a discomforting chill throughout the entire body. The darkness became suffocating, like crushing walls closing in and sucking the oxygen out of a room. They all knew sunrise would occur in the next hour or so, but the woods revealed nothing but the black of night.

A loud roar, deep enough to cause a vibration within their bodies and make the stomach rumble sent shivers of panic through the entire team. In unison, they all stumbled to the ground in kneeling positions of one sort of another. It was as if their bodies reacted to the calls in a defensive but primal way.

"Harlan, anything?" Pacer shouted, his headlamp cutting wild, chaotic patterns in the dark as he tried to see if he could spot a Bigfoot.

"Nothing," Harlan shouted back, his voice shaky. "I just want to get out of these woods."

Carl Turk, who followed behind Harlan could see his long-time acquaintance having a hard time keeping it together. He made sure to get up close to Harlan's side. "It's all right. We'll be fine. Let's just keep moving forward." Carl then asked to take Harlan's weapon, which he happily gave up.

"Keep it together. We're almost there," Pacer said trying to maintain his own composure, his hands shaking, the saliva in his throat drying up. He knew if he lost his wits, the others would most likely fall apart, maybe even break ranks and go running off into the darkness.

"But that sound was right on top of us," Alex said, his voice cracking with worry as he began to once again follow Pacer.

"Keep moving, follow me," Pacer demanded. He could feel his legs going numb, the steps awkward, stumbling because he couldn't always feel the pressure he was putting on them. It didn't help that the undulations in the terrain became more pronounced in the dark as they pushed through a sea of thick ferns. Yet he moved forward, refusing to submit to the terror trying to eat away at his nerves.

"I've got something," Harlan shouted.

"What?" Pacer shot back.

"Figures… ahead to our left," Harlan shouted back.

"How many?" Pacer asked easing his pace.

"Two, maybe three, coming right at us."

"I saw them too," Carl added, looking over Harlan's shoulder.

"Stan, get up here," Pacer barked. "I need an extra rifle."

Stan's bouncing headlamp light fluttered for a couple seconds in the dark before he showed up next to Pacer taking in deep breaths, panting with worry.

"You and Alex... aim those fucking rifles in this line," Pacer said shining his headlamp light on his arm that pointed towards the direction he wanted them to fire. "And when Harlan tells you they are within fifty yards, fire."

Stan dropped into a kneeling position and secured the rifle into his shoulder, placing his eye into the sightline looking off into the dark. Alex stood just a stride away, weapon up and ready.

"Hold steady," Pacer said as soothing as he could. He turned to Harlan. "How we doing?"

"Less than a hundred yards," Harlan answered as his best guess from years of working the devices and judging distance.

"Can you tell how many?" Pacer asked.

Harlan paused, as he watched the clumps of gray/white objects move slowly closer towards them. At times, he thought he saw three rounded tops. He wanted to say he saw three but waited. Then he noticed some separation in the figures. "Two. Moving with caution."

"Shouldn't we keep moving?" Alex asked; his voice calmer but still revealing a nervous stutter.

"Maybe you haven't noticed, but there've been no howls since we stopped," Pacer said. "I'll stay here until light if it keeps those fucking things silent and away."

"Closing in on fifty yards," Harlan said.

"Good enough," Pacer said. "Did they veer off course?"

"Not really," Harlan answered.

"Guys," Pacer shouted with force. "Fire those weapons,"

Stan couldn't feel his finger on the housing around the trigger.

"Fire it," Pacer demanded.

Stan then felt his digit tremble as it shifted over to the trigger. It felt cold. His finger wrapped itself onto the sliver of metal. He pulled back on it. It did nothing. He pulled harder. It felt locked.

"Fire damn it, one of you!" Pacer barked.

Alex froze too, not sure what paralyzed him – maybe the darkness ahead, not seeing anything at all but the shapes of a few trees.

"What are you waiting for," the others cried out, panic flooding through their voices.

This time, with more force, Stan pulled the trigger. The shot thundered, the flash from the barrel lighting the immediate area for a millisecond. Stan lost his balance on the recoil, the weapon sliding off his shoulder as he placed one arm towards the ground to catch his fall.

Without skipping a beat, Alex fired his shot, the sound vibrating hard for a moment.

Pacer felt the force of the blasts on his upper body. His head felt like it went numb. He asked Harlan what happened to the figures, hearing his own voice as if it was in a distant tunnel.

"They dropped to the ground," Harlan answered.

A distant voice began to cry out. "Cease firing."

Harlan noticed one of the figures move towards cover.

"Cease fire," the voice yelled again.

Chapter 20

Sunrise didn't produce much light in the cloudy conditions, but Chet's camp noticed they could finally make out the dark shapes of trees beyond the perimeter of their surroundings. It brought a welcome relief to the mounting tensions caused by the Sasquatch calls that had surrounded them for more than an hour. After a brief meeting, Chet, Jack, Pacer, and Sam decided enough was enough; they would end the expedition and head out as soon as they broke down the camp.

"We left our camp standing," Pacer said to the three of them.

"You want to go back and get your gear?" Jack asked, his voice frazzled.

Chet stepped in as others couldn't believe Pacer and his group worried about gear after all that unfolded. "We can wait until after sunrise... we'll all go back together and break down the camp, gather the gear and head back here. We'll pick up our stuff and head out to catch up with Bill. His group didn't have the night we had. Hopefully by then, these creatures will be out of sight."

"What if they come back?" Amy said. She was breathing heavy, anxious to get going.

Chet had no answer to placate her mood. "We're a big group. We are well equipped with guns. We'll move fast and keep our weapons spread out evenly. It shouldn't take that long. We just have to stay calm."

"When was the last time you spoke with Bill?" Alex asked.

"While you guys started arguing about the gear," Chet said. "He and the others are all about heading out as soon we get there."

"Excellent," Pacer said.

The members quickly began to break down camp while Pacer's group held watch. For a minute, the only sounds emanating from the camp were those of zippers zipping, feet shuffling about and some metallic bangs of cooking gear being organized and stuffed into backpacks. Chet and Corrine barely slid on their backpacks when a scream broke the silence around them. Not just a scream, but the primal kind that penetrates into one's deeper psyche and warns everyone of eminent danger without knowing the circumstances. They both immediately turned towards the direction of the scream. Standing just beyond the perimeter of the clearing, three dark shapes, tall, eight to ten feet in height and wide across the shoulders, appeared as silhouettes.

Amy, who was closest to the creatures and had screamed, remained motionless, kneeling next to her backpack as four more figures, larger, materialized before them, bringing the count to seven. The entire team went silent, like a standoff between prey and predator, believing that silence and stillness would make everyone invisible.

"Chet," Corrine mumbled as soft as she could, grabbing his hand. "This is it, isn't it? This is what happened to you?"

Chet said nothing at first. With a very slow movement, he raised his hand up to touch the stock of his shotgun he had slung over his shoulder. "Nothing is written yet."

"I'm frightened," she whispered.

"Yep," he answered. "But keep your head together."

"I'm trying, but I have a feeling…" she stuttered before a burst of light caught the entire camp off guard.

Harlan had taken his camera out and snapped a few pictures of the group breaking down the camp. When the Sasquatch appeared, he went to sneak a shot from chest level and accidentally triggered the camera's pop-up flash. Yet, in that brief instance, everyone caught a glimpse of what stood before them: Seven creatures, fully covered with dark brownish or rust red hair, standing between eight and twelve feet tall. They stood spaced apart in equal distribution around the bottom arc of the encampment. The creatures appeared as if giant sentinels standing guard at the gates of some secret kingdom, awaiting to hear the correct password spoken.

In the brief moment that the expedition members witnessed the Sasquatch faces, they observed figures that weren't quite ape, the jaws not as forward or pronounced as that of the typical primate. They noticed distinct features like high foreheads, a protruding nose, with a large wide bridge but proportional to the face. The attributes appeared more human than ape-like. It was hard to get a good read on the mouth area, but the lips looked rail thin or non-existent. However, it was the eyes that most zeroed in on in that brief second; dark with hints of green, hollow, set back into the skull. Chet had to squint to get a solid look, but once he did, he felt something akin to a hypnotic trance pull at his consciousness. He quickly shook it off and wondered if anyone else became enraptured in the beast's glare.

Many also noticed another feature, no eyebrows. However, the shape of the flesh rippling across the beast's faces revealed an expression of anger.

Chet knew the look and knew what was going to happen. Fixing his eyes at another beast, he once again locked eye contact as if he had no choice. As he stared deeper, he could swear that the creatures before him participated in the attack against his crew over a dozen years ago. He also knew one more thing. He was killing one of these things before they killed him. With a swiftness that caught the creatures off guard, he swung his shotgun around, positioned it at his waist, aimed at the middle grouping of creatures and fired then fired again and again.

The sound reverberated all around, crushing the silence that had permeated. The blast also acted as a starting gun as several members of the expedition began to scatter. The movement of people became a slow-motion blur to Chet. He remained focused on the creatures ahead. He hit two of them because he saw them jerk backward and stumble. One looked to fall completely to the ground.

Chet shouted for Stan and Alex to follow suit and fire. By the time either man could ready their weapon, several creatures entered the camp. Their strides brought them almost on top of some of the crew within three steps. Corrine screamed. Harlan screamed. Amy screamed, and the beasts returned their screams with louder roars, sending a pulsation through everyone's body.

One of the Sasquatches almost reached Chet when he blasted a shot into the creature's face. It blew apart - blood and chunks of skin and bones splattered back onto his face. But, one thing was certain, the creature dropped to the ground dead.

Chet turned but found himself stuck. Corrine had collapsed to the ground holding onto one of his legs like a vice grip. He turned to his left only to watch a Sasquatch grab Alex by the top of his head and yank it backward. Alex's head snapped so sharply the back of his skull touched his spine. His body went limp, falling to the forest floor, his dangling head smacking hard against the rock surface.

Chet fired a shot at the beast. The creature's body whipped back, catching the shot in the shoulder. Without a moment's hesitation, Chet fell to the ground, grabbed his fanny pack he stuffed with extra shells during the breakdown and reloaded. When Chet looked back up, one of the creatures stood over him. He spun his weapon at the creature as it lunged down at him when another shot exploded but not from his gun. The force of the fire pushed the giant beast to the ground. Stan had gotten off a shot. Chet jumped up and took a step towards the creature, dragging Corrine with him. He aimed at the beast's head and fired. It too exploded, flesh and bone splattering away from the giant body.

Looking at the splatter for just a moment, he felt a thunderous boom swat across his whole back separating him from Corrine and throwing him almost on top of the dead Bigfoot he just shot. In a daze, he turned to see one of the smaller Sasquatch's lunge towards him. The creature suddenly stopped in place and let out a pained wail, throwing its arms wildly into the air. Chet looked and saw that Amy had plunged a knife deep into the back of the beast's calf. Chet swung his rifle around to fire when he heard Amy cry out. The creature picked her up as if a toy, and threw her high into the trees. It then limped off quickly in the direction it threw her. Chet secured his rifle, fired at the fleeing Bigfoot, but nothing happened - misfire. He smacked the weapon twice and pumped it again. He stood, saw Corrine curled up on the ground, shivering like a freezing child and made his way towards her.

The creatures swarmed around the camp like brown whirlwinds, their giant swift steps crossing from one end of the camp to the next in seconds. He spotted Carl firing his weapon a couple times but could not tell if he hit anything. Screams and cries of the crew filled the air, as bodies ran frantically around him with no rhyme or reason, just the primal will to survive.

Chet turned to assess the situation. Alex laid dead, ten feet away, his head nearly separated from his body. He then spotted the cameraman, Pete, a small lake of blood pooling around where a missing arm and leg were once attached to his body. He didn't see Sam, Harlan or Amy. Only Stan, Jack, Carl, Pacer and Corrine stood inside the now eerily quiet open spot.

"What the hell was that?" Jack asked, panting heavily, eyes constantly darting around, the Sasquatch instantly disappearing from the clearing.

"That was an attack," Chet said pointing his rifle in all directions. "We should thank God more of us aren't dead. I don't understand…"

"More dead?" Pacer questioned.

"Yeah," Chet said. "They clearly could have taken us all out but didn't. It doesn't make sense."

"We need to get out of here," Corrine said, finally standing up, her voice frail. "We have to go."

"Indeed we do," Chet said as he continued to scan their surroundings.

"What about the others?" Stan asked.

"We can't go find them, we have to go, if we come across them on the way, we'll deal with it," Chet said.

"What about Amy?" Jack said, his voice frantic as he searched for her in the camp.

"She's gone," Chet said, his voice more subdued.

"Gone?" he questioned.

"Yeah... one them took her," Chet said.

"What?" Jack questioned, not understanding as he continued to look around the camp for Amy.

Chet turned to get in Jack's face, sensing he might start losing his mind. "She's gone. Get it in your head. We have to go! You want to deal with that again? Next time it could be you." Chet had barely finished when Carl fired a shot, then a second. Chet watched a creature swarm over Carl, grabbing him, smacking the weapon out of hands then taking off with his body tucked under its arm as if he was nothing more than a football.

Chet turned to Corrine whose face was white with fright. "It's time to go. There's nothing we can do for him now."

Corrine blinked a couple times as if her body was trying to make an electrical connection. "I'm following you," she murmured.

"One thing first," Chet said as he rushed over to Pete. He bent down, grabbed the camera that lay only a foot away from the dead body and pulled out the memory card. "This should seal the deal." He saw Corrine standing by Amy's backpack and told her to get the video camera.

Corrine nodded, still half in a daze. She opened a side pouch and to her miraculous delight, found the camera in it.

Chet turned to the others. "Pacer… get Alex's rifle, Jack grab Carl's," Chet said while taking hold of Corrine's hand.

Chet called for the others to get ready to move out. Then, just as the group stepped into the still dark woods, another series of howls erupted, but this time, they could locate the direction – from their rear and closing in.

"Let's double time this now," Chet barked.

The faint light that aided their vision in the open encampment area now had almost completely vanished inside the thick of the woods. Not quite the pitch black of earlier, they still needed the aid of headlamps of which only Chet and Stan had on. The others lost theirs in the melee. Corrine, much to her surprise, had a small LED flashlight in her pocket. It didn't produce much coverage but any light that could help with seeing their footing became an added bonus.

Again, another call filled the air, followed by a second roar coming from their rear. A couple seconds later, a distant but distinct answering call came from their front. Chet slowed, if only to make sure he heard the direction of the sounds correctly. He took out his radio and began calling for Bill. No answer came. *Shit.*

"Do you think they came under attack?" Corrine asked, not really wanting to know the answer.

"I don't know," Chet, answered, keeping his pace, dead branches crashing against his shins as he plowed through unseen forest clutter.

"Then why haven't they returned your call?" Jack asked, his voice cracking, his breathing heavy.

"I have no idea," Chet said, getting annoyed at the inquiry and having no possible answer for anyone. He did fear Bill's camp fell under attack, but admitting it would only lead to his group having bigger panic issues. "We just have to keep moving. When we get closer, we'll assess the situation."

Chet took another couple steps before the ground disappeared beneath him. Lurching forward, he fell, tumbling down a small slope. He slapped at the ground trying to dig his fingers into it, but the soft soil just slipped away. Within seconds he came to a stop.

Corrine shouted for him. She was only able to see his spinning headlamp twirl in the dark. When the light came to a stop, she shined what little light her flashlight produced and could see that they had come to the slope that led to the Sasquatch structures. Stan took his more powerful light and located Chet who began to rise up on his feet.

"You alright?" Corrine asked.

"I'm fine," he returned seeing their lights shine on him. "Let's go. Just be careful."

Chet watched the lights bounce down the slope and could hear the hushed demands of 'be careful.' It took a minute for the four of them to descend. Chet walked over to the gathering group. "Let's see if we can spot that structure."

Stan started a slow pan of the woods with his light. The heavy cloud cover kept the morning light from making more of an impact. Slowly though, their field of vision grew so they could see about fifty feet with little issue.

"Shit," Stan whispered as his lone light passed by a portion of the squatch structure.

"Right there," Jack said pointing, his breath beginning to pant. "Oh my God."

At the top of the dimming range of their lights, Jack spotted feet dangling.

"Raise the light up. Don't you see it?" Jack asked.

As soon as Stan and Chet raised their lights a bit, two bodies appeared before them. They couldn't tell at first who it was. The distance was too far.

"Oh my goodness," Corrine said as she brought her hand to her mouth. She began to cry.

"What?" Chet asked using one arm to bring her closer to him.

"One of them is Amy," she murmured.

Jack jerked his head towards Corrine at hearing Amy's name. He then began to walk closer to the bodies.

"No Jack, wait," Chet said in vain, his words falling flat.

Stan followed. Chet ushered Corrine along bringing up the rear.

Jack's body became more of a shape in the dark as he trotted ahead. A second later, they heard him scream and drop to his knees.

Looking up, they could see that a long thick branch impaled Amy from the lower back up through her torso, the point coming out just below the sternum. The branch smashed right through her spine, propping her body up straight. Only Amy's head slumped forward, her chin nearly resting on her chest. On closer inspection, Chet noticed a slow but steady trickling of blood falling from her shoes to the forest floor.

"And that's Carl," Pacer gasped. His impaled body propped up by another thick branch only a couple feet away from Amy's. It wasn't the body or face that gave his identity away but the bright neon green pants and distinctive black and red vest he often wore on expeditions.

"Okay, we gotta get the fuck out of here, and we have to do it now," Chet said with urgency as he tapped Jack's shoulder to bring him out of his daze.

"Look what they did to my Amy," Jack mumbled, still on his knees, crying.

Chet knew full well what happened. "I know... we have to go."

Jack didn't move; his body just swaying around like a fishing bobber on a lake. Chet moved towards him to jerk him up when another guttural call followed by another then a third rose up and surrounded them, sending vibrations through their bodies.

"Guys, Chet, anyone... can you hear me?" a voice crackled.

Chet, at first, looked all around not sure where the static sounding voice came from before realizing it was his radio. "Check, Chet here."

"Thank God Chet, it's Bill, where the hell are you?"

Chapter 21

"What the hell are we going to do Bill?" Nathan Avent, a former grad student of Bill's and youngest member of the research crew, asked as he held a hunting knife that visibly shook in his hand.

"I just got contact with Chet," Bill shot back, his voice harried. "We have to remain as calm as possible. We have help coming."

"And exactly what are they going to do against these things?" Avery asked, his back to Bill, body shaking, keeping an eye out on the perimeter to see if he could spot anymore Sasquatch.

Bill ran his fingers through his disheveled hair pulling a few strands out, hardly even noticing. His breathing had calmed some, but he could still feel his heart pumping at a rapid rate, the pulse pounding in his neck, ears, and wrist, not to mention his chest. "They have weapons. It's added gunfire."

Bill's group had two rifles, one of them his. Jeff Cass held the other one, but his experience with it wasn't much. Jeff had never hunted before, only firing his new Savage 16/116 bolt action a few times at an outdoor range. When Jack called him to join the expedition, he volunteered to bring his rifle in case they ran into a Grizzly or Mountain Lion. Having been on several expeditions, he never thought he would actually have to use it. He just liked the idea of having one.

"How are you doing Jeff?" Bill shouted.

Jeff stood on the far side of the encampment from where Bill stood. The Bigfoot had shown themselves twice. The first encounter saw two creatures run through the camp smashing down the tents in their path before vanishing back into the woods. To Bill, the actions reminded him of something akin to a primate's behavior in protecting its own territory. The creatures didn't seem to want to bring harm as they vanished back into the shadows.

It was the second encounter with the creatures that turned chaotic and fatal. A few minutes after first disappearing back into the forest, several shapes appeared once again just beyond the periphery of the camp. The creatures shifted around, bobbing in and out of the cover darkness. Jeff became overly nervous after the beasts began to howl. When one of the creatures penetrated the imaginary boundary of the camp's site, Jeff fired two shots at it. At least one of the bullets hit. The creature turned, roared then grabbed Zachary who had the unfortunate luck of being closest to the beast when Jeff shot it. The Sasquatch plucked Zachary up like he was a salt shaker on a dinner table, and twisted his head in a complete circle. No screams ever came from Zachary as the creature slipped back into the darkness.

"We're out of the Squatch Structures and on our way," Chet said over the radio.

"Hurry," Bill said as he thought he noticed at least two other Bigfoot lurking deeper in the shadows. He sensed the Sasquatch knew exactly how close they could get to the clearing without revealing more of themselves than just faint shapes.

"I see something," Jeff shrieked. "They're back."

Bill and Nathan turned towards Jeff and could see his whole body shake. Indeed, several tall figures presented themselves just beyond the border of their encampment. They counted five.

"Easy Jeff," Bill pleaded.

Jeff jerked the stock of the rifle up into his shoulder, raised the barrel towards the figures. "Get the fuck out of here," he yelled at the creatures. "Leave us alone. We'll go, just leave us alone."

The figures simply stood still. Not a single movement in their stances as if they were stone shapes in the environment. Bill could barely make out their outlines. With the light of day slowly revealing more and more landscape, the Sasquatches stood further away from the clearing.

"Don't do anything hasty, Jeff," Bill implored trying to ease his nervous companion. "They seem to have heard you. Whether they actually understood you is another matter, but you certainly got their attention."

"They just have to go back," Jeff countered, still keeping the rifle up and aimed into the woods. "They give us space, let us leave, then I don't have to fire this thing. But if they make a charge, I'm shooting every round I have."

"I really don't know how effective that rifle is going to be," Bill said as he moved his hand slowly to make sure his shotgun clung to his back.

"Well... we won't know if he doesn't fire," Nathan shot back in support of Jeff.

"I hit one of those bastards before," Jeff yelled. "And they went away."

"I don't know about that Jeff," Bill said.

"I'm certainly not going to stop him if he tries Bill," Avery said. Avery had kept mostly quiet and low, hoping the creatures wouldn't notice him.

"What the fuck Bill? Are you on their side or something?" Jeff screamed, his voice quivering with fear. "If I knew I could kill them, I'd shoot every one of these mother fuckers right now."

"We certainly hope that doesn't need to happen," Bill countered. "Let's just try to keep our wits about us." Bill hoped Chet and the others would arrive soon. He didn't think he could contain Jeff's precarious mental state much longer, especially if Jeff interpreted the creature's moves as threatening.

"All they have to do is make one move forward, and I'm firing," Jeff said.

"Think about that for a moment Jeff," Bill said as if he was a professional negotiator. "You only have one shot at a time, you're nervous, unsteady. It's not like you have a shotgun. You can easily miss with that thing and only piss them off more."

"So what are you saying Bill," Avery barked. "We're to wait until we see the whites of their eyes? They took Zachary. He's gone. I say Jeff shoots the moment they make a move on us. What about your gun? Why don't you use it? If you aren't, then give it to me."

"Guys please," Bill said, pleading, feeling the situation slipping away.

"No Bill," Avery shot back. But before he could say anymore, a nine-foot-tall, dark beast came rushing into the camp from their rear and grabbed Avery by the back of his jacket and lifted him into his arms. Avery screamed, the shriek exuding every ounce of helpless terror a soul could muster.

Jeff turned to see the beast streaking towards him. He aimed his rifle at the creature's abdomen and fired. The shot missed, and the beast continued its quick stride, disappearing back into the shelter of the forest.

"Nathan!" Bill shouted seeing the young man slump to the ground. He ran towards him only a few feet away seeing Nathan clutch at his chest.

When Bill slid up next to him, he could see Nathan was still breathing, but with quick, labored breaths, his eyes blinking as if stunned, not sure exactly what just happened. Blood oozed from his torso, quickly soaking through all his clothes.

"Oh my God, I killed Nathan," Jeff said stumbling towards them while dropping his weapon.

Bill could see the quiver in Jeff's lips, the wide-eyed shock in his eyes, tears streaming down his cheeks. "You can't blame yourself for this," Bill said, choking back vomit while trying to remain calm. "You tried to protect us."

Jeff fell on top of Nathan's body and clawed at his jacket screaming how sorry he was and pleading for the young man not to die.

Bill knew Nathan was as good as dead. It came down to a matter of minutes before the young man would bleed out. The only good thing to come of it, Bill thought, was that Nathan quickly fell into shock and probably had no conscious awareness of his fate.

"They're still there," Jeff said when he looked up from Nathan's body. "They're still fucking there," he yelled. Jeff then stood up and screamed. Panting heavily, he spotted his rifle and bolted towards it. Right before he could pick it up, another Sasquatch, not quite as big as the previous one, ran out from the cover of the woods. Jeff never saw the beast approach until the very last second when the Sasquatch's forearm swung towards him. A crushing blow pulsated through his body, his sternum collapsing while his body left the ground. A moment later, his back crashed against a tree, falling to the ground, barely conscious.

Bill watched the Sasquatch run towards Jeff's slumped over body. The creature lifted Jeff up and swung his body like a baseball bat against a tree, repeating the motion several times before letting Jeff's limp body drop onto a flat slab of rock.

Bill froze. He lost all feeling in his limbs. The sight of Jeff's head swinging loose like a ball on a string while the beast beat him against the tree was all he needed to witness to know Jeff had expired. Bill now sat alone. "Where are those guys?"

Chapter 22

"I can see a clearing ahead," Chet said, his voice filling with excitement. Enough light filled the woods that they could all easily see over a hundred feet with relative ease.

"Then maybe we can get the hell out of here once and for all," Corrine chimed in with a hint of relief.

"Let's get them and head out," Jack added. "They can fill us in on their experience while we get the fuck out of here."

As the five came closer to the clearing, Chet gave a shout to let Bill and company know they were approaching. Chet feared a nervous trigger finger just like Pacer's group had earlier. He gave a second shout out. Not hearing an immediate response, he slowed his pace.

"Bill, it's us, we're coming closer, keep your weapons down," Chet shouted then repeated the same into the radio.

They were less than a hundred feet when Bill's voice came back with a faint reply none of them could decipher.

"Keep your weapon low," Chet said to Stan. "Let me go in first, follow a few feet behind."

Stan, Pacer, and Jack backed off, but Corrine grabbed at Chet's jacked, squeezed the material and told him she wasn't leaving his side.

Chet knew better than to argue with her. "Bill, Bill, Bill," Chet repeated as the two of them walked closer to the opening. Chet finally could see a figure, the person's back was to him, and they appeared to be sitting. "Bill," Chet cried out.

Bill turned towards them. Chet could see tears streaming down his friend's face. His stomach immediately tightened, and he knew something had gone horribly wrong.

"What happened Bill?" Chet asked as he kneeled closer to his friend. He hadn't finished his question when he spotted the body of Nathan on the ground next to Bill, blood pooling on the dirt.

"Jeff accidentally shot him," Bill said trying to control his crying.

"Where's Jeff?" Corrine asked placing a comforting hand on Bill's shoulder.

Bill pointed in an adjacent direction without looking. "Over there by that tree."

Corrine stood to see while Chet craned his neck. Both saw Jeff's body lying motionless.

"What happened? Why is he over there?" Chet asked. "Where are the others?"

Bill shook his head, and the tears came on strong. "Something... one of those... I don't know... smashed him against a tree like a guitar against a wall... then dropped him."

"What? Why?" Corrine said kneeling back down.

"Jeff tried to shoot them, and they attacked," Bill said gaining a touch of composure.

"You've been attacked?" asked Corrine before she realized how foolish the question sounded.

Bill cocked his head, his eyebrows raising, "And you haven't?"

"Attacked? We've lost at least six people that we know of," Chet said. "A few of those things overran the camp, and some people ran off. We have no idea what happened to them."

"Three died here in a matter of minutes," Bill said. "Zachary died first... at least I think. They took him, and we heard nothing. After that Jeff, Nathan and Avery were killed like boom, boom, boom, one right after the other."

"Yeah, well we're getting out of here now," Jack said as he, Pacer and Stan walked into the camp and took defensive positions. Jack spotted the rifle on the ground. "Was that Jeff's?"

Bill nodded.

"Well, it's ours now. We're getting out of this death trap," Pacer said as he walked towards the rifle.

"No," Bill called out.

Pacer stopped. "Why, What?"

"When Jeff picked up his rifle to aim at them, they came out like a rush of wind and destroyed him."

"Where are they?" Stan asked as he eyed the surroundings, jerking his rifle from point to point around the camp.

"They were just into the woods, beyond where we could see them well," Bill said pointing in the direction where he had seen the Sasquatch.

All of them looked in the general direction that Bill pointed towards.

"I don't see anything now," Pacer said as he began a cautious approach to the rifle, keeping one eye on the woods.

The others began a feverish appraisal of their surroundings looking for any shape that might resemble a Bigfoot. The new day's light, slow in coming, kept revealing more of the landscape. Looking in every direction, none of them could make a definitive identification of the creatures.

"Looks clear," Stan said as he watched Pacer stand over the rifle.

Pacer bent down nice and easy as he continued to look off into the depths of the woods. He tapped the ground several times feeling for the weapon before finally touching it. Clutching it, he brought it to his side and slowly stood up.

"I see nothing; do you guys see anything?" Jack asked.

All of them said no.

"Okay then," Chet said as he stood up. "Let's get out of here."

They all left the clearing but as soon as they stepped into the woods, a chorus of calls and howls erupted around them once again as if signaling that the humans were on the move. The screeches and howls pressed against their senses, suffocating them, making them wince and clutch at their bellies.

Chet urged the group on but could see how the penetrating sounds affected them as if they each suddenly came down with horrid stomach cramps. "We have to continue. Get past it," he admonished seeing Stan and Jack begin to stumble as they walked.

Still, the others waivered. There wide mouthed expressions revealed they had as much as they could handle of the terrible howls that filled the forest and chiseled away at their bones.

Chet looked at Corrine. She was crying, falling to the ground and curling up into a fetal position. "What are you doing?" he called out to her and the others. "Move it, move it or we're all dead. Come on! On your feet."

His demands seemed to take hold as if his voice had the power to break a spell. Slowly, they began to move forward, stumbling at first before becoming upright.

Chet continually looked over his shoulder to make sure everyone followed. If any one of them broke ranks and ran off, he was certain it would be that person's doom.

Chet couldn't understand why the last set of calls distressed the group so much. It didn't affect him. He wondered if the pitch of the calls or the vibrations caused some kind of disturbance that rendered its victims helpless, allowing the creatures to easily attack its prey.

Chet pushed through the thickening underbrush. He continued to encourage everyone to move forward. The mental and physical anguish of the night was really beginning to takes its toll on the surviving members.

There was no way he was stopping or letting any of them stop. He now had proof of an attack. He made sure to procure Pete's camera's memory card and held onto the video camera Corrine took out of Amy's backpack. Bigfoot was real, and the world would see it once and for all. Using that thought as fuel, he pushed on with all his energy.

Suddenly, Corrine began to scream. "Nooooo."

Chet and the others searched around, twisting their bodies and heads to see what terrified Corrine so much. Jack spotted the source. He fell silent, falling to his knees with exhaustion, his hope slipping away. Chet noticed it last as he attended to Corrine, trying to comfort her hysteria.

Hanging from a series of branches about a hundred feet away and thirty feet above with arms and legs stretched wide, one of their crew hung skinless. The entire body remained intact, but every last shred of the outer layer of skin had been peeled off like someone skinned a catfish. Looking closer at the naked body, droplets of blood streamed to the forest floor. No one could quite tell who it was, but Jack and Pacer guessed it was Harlan because of his more rounded belly.

"It's a trap," Chet said. "We have to continue moving."

Jack began to vomit, and as soon as the sound of his digested food splashed against the ground, Corrine followed suit, then Stan. The sight made Chet's stomach twist into knots, and he could feel the acids churning. He turned away, took a deep breath and worked on trying to compose himself. He knew he had to keep it together. If he lost his wits, they would all die.

Chet pleaded that they needed to go when he caught sight of a figure moving their way. At first, he thought it might be a Sasquatch, but it looked too small. The frame didn't have the girth for a Bigfoot. As the body moved closer, he noticed it was Sam. Sam had run off in the initial melee when the creatures first began their assault.

"Sam? Is that you?" Chet called out.

The figure said nothing as it stumbled closer, still very much a silhouette in the dark cover of the woods. Jack called out, and Sam motioned with a weak wave. Jack ran to him. Sam fell into his embrace as if Jack had arrived just in time to catch him.

Stan and Pacer couldn't believe it. Corrine finally calmed

down as a small smile of relief crawled across her face.

"Where the hell have you been?" Jack said as he embraced Sam then looked back at the crew with amazement.

"Running," Sam choked out, his voice sounding dry and cracked.

"We're getting the hell out of here," Jack said before he felt something stop him where he stood. He looked at Sam, whose mouth was open but no words came, just a vacant stare in his eyes. Jack all of a sudden, began to lose his eyesight as the world became blurry around him. He felt consciousness slipping away. There was no pain. His knees gave out and he began falling down with Sam in his arms. Just before he hit the ground, he heard a faint cry of terror echoing off in the distance.

Corrine screamed louder than she ever had, the pitch actually hurting Chet's ear where he had to let go of her. Her scream didn't cease, echoing all around them just like the Sasquatch calls had. She noticed a large figure hurl something. It was a long branch, roughed hewn to a point. The spear-like object penetrated through Sam's spine and abdomen and went straight into Jack's body, the point of the branch protruding out of Jack's back.

"Run!" yelled Chet as he watched his two friends lay on the ground. He reached over to Corrine, grabbed the back of her sweater and yanked her into moving. "Stan, Bill, Pacer, let's go," he shouted.

In his haste to leave the scene, Chet lost his bearings. He searched the woods as he ran. As long as he didn't go uphill, they were fine. He desperately looked for a down slope. He knew they should come to one soon.

Corrine continued to cry. Chet had to pull her along and keep her focused, her steps awkward and clumsy. Stan ran just a few strides behind, his breathing labored but able to keep pace. Bill followed, and Pacer took the rear, constantly peering over his shoulder to see if any of the Sasquatch chased after them.

As much as it pained him, Chet had to stop after what he guessed was at least seventy-five yards of a full out run. He needed to catch his breath and get his bearings in order. The forest had brightened considerably. He could see quite far ahead, at least several hundred feet with no issues. He needed to find the downward slope. He knew it was nearby. He couldn't remember hiking over this much flat surface.

"Over there," Corrine said pointing to where several trees branches looked lower in appearance.

Chet nodded. "As good as anything. Let's go."

Several strides into their run, Bill began shouting that he spotted a couple of Sasquatch parallel to them either trying to cut them off or tracking them.

Chet scanned as he ran. He saw nothing, just the woods. "Where?" Chet shouted slowing down just a touch.

"To my right, at least three," Pacer shot back having seen the same thing.

"I didn't see anything," Corrine added.

"Just keep moving. We'll deal with it when it presents itself," Chet said, once again picking up the pace of the run over the soft forest floor, bashing through groves of thick ferns.

The five of them came to the slope Corrine had pointed out. Pausing to assess the steepness, Chet worried they might not be able to handle the harshness of the grade; it wasn't the same topography they had climbed earlier. Chet knew one stumble on this grade, and it could lead to an uncontrollable fall. The slope before them needed a slow, careful descent, an aspect of getting away he didn't think they had the luxury of having.

"What do you think?" Corrine huffed as she peered down the drop, seeing a blur of trees coming straight into their site line.

Shooting a quick glance along the line of the slope, Chet knew they had little choice. "This is our only chance until it isn't. We have to maneuver it as best we can."

Stan had his hands on his hips, rifle slung over his shoulder as he took in deep breaths. "Then what are we waiting for?"

"Nothing," Chet said gritting his teeth at the challenge ahead of them. "Just be careful." With that, Chet led, turning his body to handle the slope from a sideways position.

Hiking always has its subtle dangers, whether animal, washed out trails, downed trees blocking passage, sprained ankles, a bad fall, but bushwhacking multiplied those dangers by a factor of ten, with the added bonus of getting lost. Chet worried about another nuance, the stability of the ground. Trails are hard packed surfaces, well-worn and solid footing for the most part. In the middle of the woods, the forest floor often tended towards soft and at times slippery with moist needles, leaves, and small sticks. Maintaining good footholds and balance played an important part in successful backwoods bushwhacking. He imagined the hidden potholes of the forest; those dips in the ground that could twist an ankle or worse, break one. Stepping into one could also lead to a nasty fall, which of course, on this slope would most likely lead to either a major injury or possibly death.

"Careful now as we go down," Chet cautioned. "One slip here and you won't have to worry about a Sasquatch attack, the fall will kill you."

Corrine, Stan, Bill and Pacer shuffled their feet impatiently, staring at Chet with dumbfounded expressions at his slow approach.

Stan had no patience for the pace. "I'm just getting the hell outta here, and I'm gonna do it as quick as I can," he said as he began his climb down. After a few steps, his momentum picked up, quickly passing by Chet.

"Careful," Chet pleaded seeing Stan's dangerous pace. He turned to Corrine and stretched out an arm. "Ready?"

She nodded. Without taking Chet's aid, she began her decent. Pacer and Bill followed.

They hadn't gone down fifteen steps when the forest erupted with howls. Once again, they came from all directions, surrounding the five of them, casting an invisible veil over their climb down.

Chet turned to see Stan picking up speed and called out for him to stop. Stan didn't, he just kept shuffling down the slope. Then it happened. Stan lost his balance. As if in slow motion, Stan fell forward and began to tumble. First, his shoulders and head slammed into the ground, followed by his legs pinwheeling above his body, looking like a bad cartwheel as he hurtled down the slope.

"Stan!" Corrine yelled, the small lines on her face deepening as she watched in horror. She called again but didn't think Stan could hear her.

The four froze as they helplessly watched Stan spin down the hill, a limp mass, twisting and careening off trees like a pinball until he fell out of view. Another call erupted followed by others. This time, the calls came from below them in the direction where Stan tumbled. Chet thought he saw a flash of something large and dark bolt between the trees in the distance. A couple seconds later, they heard Stan's screams cut through the forest, and as quickly as they heard him, a dead silence followed.

"What now?" Corrine huffed, anxiety taking over, her shoulders and chest heaving with bigger and bigger panicked breaths.

"We keep going," Chet said as he examined the forest for anything that resembled a usable path.

"Where? That way?" Corrine gasped as she pointed in the direction where Stan fell.

Giving the landscape another quick study, Chet noticed a slightly less radical decline if they took an approach to their left. "This way," he said grabbing her wrist and changing the angle of their descent.

"Are you sure," she said following his lead with no resistance.

He wasn't, but it was his best guess. "Yes."

Chet slid his feet along the ground, barely lifting them off the surface, always careful of the footing. He also maintained a steady pace, not fast and certainly not too slow.

The land began to level out after another hundred yards of shuffling. He turned to look at Corrine, Bill, and Pacer. Corrine's stare let him know she had concentrated hard on not falling. He came to a stop next to a wider than average tree. Taking in deep breaths of air, he asked how the three were holding up. Corrine nodded and said she was fine. Pacer and Bill worked on catching their collective breaths while giving a thumbs up.

"Do you hear that?" Pacer said as he jerked his head around trying to locate the source of a sound.

Chet did not. "What?"

Pacer put up a finger to wait. A couple seconds later, a small grin took over his face. "I hear water... a river."

Chet couldn't hear it. He craned his head in the direction that Pacer pointed but heard nothing. "Can't hear it."

"I hear it," Corrine chirped like a teenage girl finding out a boy who she liked, liked her too.

"I think I do too," Bill said.

"Then let's go towards it," Chet said and continued down the mountain.

Several more minutes passed. Their quads and calves began to scream in agony. The force of having to steady their momentum and not go too fast wore on all their legs and knees. They had to take a quick break for fear of losing balance in a weakened state.

Chet then shot up straight, his body stiff; his head looking around like a deer would after hearing a suspicious sound. "I hear it."

Corrine stood up tall. She cocked her head about before stopping and smiling again. "I hear it too."

"We're not too far from it either," Pacer said, feeling they were finally close to escaping the mountain.

Corrine nodded and lifted her back away from the tree. "Let's go."

Again, the four continued their shuffle down the slope. Bill suddenly cried out in agony after about twenty yards. When the others turned to see what happened, Bill lay on the ground, writhing in pain, grabbing at his leg. He slid into a depression, his boot catching and with the weight of his momentum, snapping his tibia, resulting in a compound fracture. Bill could do little but cry out.

Chet for the first time felt completely helpless. He knew instantly they couldn't help him. Yet, looking at his friend squirm in pain, squeezing his face muscles to not scream so loud, Chet could not abandon his friend either. Out of instinct, the three of them went towards Bill. Chet glanced at the leg, part of it still in the ground at close to a ninety-degree angle, the rest of him lying down.

"Bill?" Chet gasped not sure what to say.

"Chet," Bill managed to spit out. "Go. I'm finished."

"I can't," Chet said beginning to cry for the first time.

Bill lunged his body towards Chet, grabbed his jacket and pulled him down on top of him. "You listen to me. Get the hell out of here." With every word Bill uttered, streams of spit followed. "I'm dead. I can act as a distraction. I'll call out. They'll come for me and with any mercy maybe they'll kill me quickly."

"No!" Chet barked.

"Then what," Bill said, his voice weakening. "We all die here?" He let go of Chet's jacket, falling away, crying in agony and resignation. "But first, take my phone… inside my top jacket pocket... I have pictures of the casts I made, the footprints, video capturing the howls, maybe even one or two them standing outside our camp. Take it."

Chet reached over and took the phone.

"Go," Bill spit out.

"But Bill," Chet mumbled.

"Fucking Go damn it," Bill shouted as he tried once again to prop himself up. "Before I pass out, let me help you. I've got this gun. Let me shoot one of those things. I might be able to give you guys an extra minute or two to get away."

Another round of howls erupted.

"See, they are closing in... go!" Bill demanded.

Chet stood up. He felt numb, not sure what to say.

A single giant roar reverberated, snapping Chet back into the present. All Chet could do was nod. "Thank you my friend." With that, Chet turned, grabbed Corrine who silently sobbed and motioned for Pacer to follow.

Not thirty seconds into leaving Bill's side they heard Bill call out to the Sasquatch to come get him. He spat out a bunch of profanity as he called the beasts every derogatory name he could think of at that moment.

Several roars followed. Bill's voice became fainter as they continued down the mountain. Another roar erupted. Shots fired. Then one pained scream echoed for a moment, followed by silence.

Chet staggered as he cursed knowing his friend sacrificed his life for them.

"It's going to be okay baby," Corrine said with a soothing tone as she now held Chet steady, his knees buckling, his body wavering.

In less than a minute, they could hear rushing water above the sound of their feet sliding and stomping on the forest floor. Chet continued a little further before coming to another stop. He scanned their setting. "Come on, we're almost there."

The land lessened its decline again. They began to walk facing forward. Chet picked up the speed, weaving in and out of the tree line so they could move faster without going in a dangerous straight line.

"A clearing ahead," Pacer said.

Corrine beamed. "We're really going to make it."

Chet didn't respond to her declaration. He knew they still had a while to go and wouldn't rest until they launched boats and made it out onto the lake. Slowing his pace, his stomach began to turn, a new rush of adrenaline poured through him. He slowed to a walk, grabbed Corrine's hand as the three of them saw a bright opening in the landscape. Staring ahead, no trees existed, just distance. Chet knew what they were coming to. His heart suddenly sank. Stepping past the last series of trees, he looked out to see they stood at the mountain's edge - a small bare cut out followed by a sheer drop cliff. He looked down. A river flowed below. He guessed at least a seventy-five-foot fall, maybe more.

"This can't be it," Corrine said with dismay.

"Shit," Pacer said through clenched teeth.

Looking towards the downward slope of the mountain, Chet could see they still had quite a distance to go. It did, after all, take a full day's climb to get to the first campsite, and they had only been heading downhill for about ninety minutes. Yet given the pace, he knew they were making fine progress but not enough that they would see the road anytime soon.

"I thought we were so much closer," Corrine whispered. "We have to be closer than this."

Chet didn't know how to console her. He couldn't, there were no words. He then spotted a sliver of blue in the distance. "Look," he said, turning her towards the blue mark in the distance.

"What?" she said, not noticing at first.

"Hill Creek Lake," Chet said with enthusiasm. "We're getting there."

"About time," Pacer added with relief.

The site brought some consolation to Corrine. She glanced down at the river. It appeared big, but she couldn't really tell anything more about it.

Chet turned to her. He touched her face, leaned in and gave her a kiss. She returned the embrace, wrapping her arms around his back. Pulling away, he whispered into her ear. "We're doing this."

Corrine breathed a sigh of relief. "Then let's."

Walking back into the woods, they only took a few steps before freezing in their tracks. Standing before them, five giant Sasquatches. Their width and spacing looked to cover over thirty feet. The dark beasts stood tall, shoulders wide and arms away from their bodies as if someone placed giant softballs in their armpits.

"Oh my God no," Corrine yelled with a ferocious force. Her body began to tremble.

The creatures at first reacted with a slight jerk, surprised by the sudden shriek. A moment later, all five returned the scream with their own howls, vibrating the ground all around.

Chet felt remarkably at ease. He stared into the dark eyes of the Bigfoot. He could see they were looking at him, his unwavering glare. Chet could have sworn one of them twitched their eyes as if it recognized him. He shook his head at the creature. "Not today you bastards."

The five creatures took a giant step towards the three of them, now less than twenty-five feet away. Chet could see how towering and menacing the beasts appeared. These weren't the creatures that people have fuzzy video of or the shadows of figures walking casually off-frame from great distances. These beings stood tall, unafraid, almost zombie-like in their stoic expressions. Chet noticed they didn't seem to blink, their dark eyes just glaring, studying.

Chet pulled out Bill's phone, the video recorder and memory card he had in his jacket. He looked at Corrine, her face vacant, her body shivering. "It's your time honey," he snapped, making sure she heard him.

She glanced towards him. "What?"

He stretched out his hand with the items. "Take these. It's the proof of what we have done here."

"What are you talking about?" Corrine said, her voice shaking. "No."

"I have to hold these things off. This is my destiny, right here," Chet said staring deeply into her eyes.

"No," she answered, barely able to get the response out.

"Take them," Chet insisted, stuffing the phone and memory card in her pants pocket then making sure she grabbed hold of the video recorder. "Jump off that cliff. Do it! The river below will catch you right. It's deep enough."

She looked back towards the cliff, then him. "How do you know that?"

"The big pool where the rushing water goes into, it's deep, and it's right below us. Go feet first." He wasn't actually certain, but it was her only hope of survival. He could see the creatures slowly creeping in towards them, taking their time, like they knew they had their prey captured. "The three of us can't fit into that pool all at once," he said taking another glance down towards it. "We might be able to hold them off, but you can certainly survive that drop. Once out, follow the river down the mountain, it'll bring you to the lake. I'll follow if I can, but you have to go."

Chet caught Pacer out of the corner of his eye bringing his rifle up and pointed it at the beasts.

Pacer took a few steps towards the creatures. "Fuck you, you bastards. I'm taking a few of you out before you get your due with me." He pulled the trigger. Nothing happened. "Oh no," he mumbled.

In an instant one of the creatures leaped forward, grabbed Pacer from where he stood like he was a doll, turned back towards the woods, and ran, vanishing in seconds. Pacer screamed for a moment, then, nothing.

"Oh my God," Corrine screamed.

Chet grit his teeth, turned to her knowing time was running out. "Go Now!"

"I can't do it without you," she cried.

"You're going to have to," Chet said. "You can do it. You're strong enough, always have been."

"Chet, no, no, not without you."

"I'll hold them off, let you get in the water. I'll follow. You have to do it now, or neither one of us will get out of here alive," Chet said, securing his shotgun in both hands and swinging it up to his hip, motioning the barrel towards each one of the remaining Sasquatch.

"No," she whimpered.

"Yes," he yelled. "Now, damn it!" With that, the beasts stepped closer. One more step and they would expose themselves to the open area.

Chet shuffled his feet back another foot, almost at the cliff's edge. "Go!"

Corrine felt flush, her face becoming numb. She watched one of the beasts step out from the shadows of the trees. Not knowing how, or why, she ran two steps towards the cliff, never hesitating, and jumped with all her strength.

Chet only caught a glimpse of her disappearing, but a grin stretched across his face. He turned back to the beasts who now stood, at most, fifteen feet away.

"Long time no see, boys," Chet said as he calmly raised his weapon higher, put one of the Bigfoot in his sight line then fired. The creature he aimed at fell to the ground. He fired again. The shot hit another Bigfoot but did not kill it. Looking down the barrel of his shotgun, he noticed the beast squint and curl its thin lip upwards, expressing a deep anger. He fired another shot, dropping the creature. Before he could get off a fourth shot, a powerful force slammed into the side of his face. Everything went dark, darker than any night he'd ever experienced.

Corrine screamed as she fell, her environment flying by in blurs. She heard gun shots, faint and fading. Then her feet hit the water. Her legs collapsed into her chest. She sucked in water as she descended into the pool flailing away with her arms to stop the rush of water that streamed up her nose and clothes. Her feet touched the bottom with a thud, but not with any kind of overly forceful impact. Feeling the sandy bottom briefly, she pushed off and propelled herself to the surface.

Coming out of the water, she gasped for air. Turning in several directions to get her bearings, she looked up to where she jumped from. It seemed much further away than the couple seconds it took to hit the water. She couldn't even rightly identify the exact spot she jumped from.

"Chet," she called out. She waited, but no one answered. The world remained silent. Treading water, she began to feel the river slowly carry her downstream. With relative ease, she paddled to the far shore of the river then pulled herself out.

Once on land, she began to take in long deep breaths while laying on the grassy shoreline. She looked up. She couldn't see anything but trees, as she once again tried to locate where she jumped from. Then came howls. Several calls echoed through the air. They seemed different this time, almost as if they were pissed off. Pissed that they let one go.

Placing her hand on the ground to push herself up, she realized she still held the video recorder in her hand. Gasping, she began to slap at her pockets until she felt the shape of the phone and memory card. Pulling each out, she hoped they weren't ruined. She managed to turn on Bill's phone. Corrine breathed a brief sigh of relief until she realized, she was now alone. Pulling her knees into her chest while seated, she began to sway back and forth crying as she came to grips with her circumstance.

When another lone howl erupted from a different direction than the mountain, it caught her attention. Looking around, she spotted what appeared to be a path of sorts then ran down it, then down another long slope, not stopping until she came to a service road. Breathing hard, she stopped and sat for a couple of minutes. Tears welled up in her eyes once again. However, this time, she didn't weep uncontrollably. She wiped at her tears, put her face in her hands and just tried to breathe deeply. She knew she wasn't free of the beasts just yet.

A horn blew. Corrine looked up. A forest service pickup truck slowly approached. As it came closer, she could see the driver's side window roll down.

"Ma'am?" the young worker said, who looked like he was in his early twenties, confused to see a woman in the middle of nowhere. "You okay?"

Corrine sniffed, and tried to control her crying. "No, but thank God you are here."

Epilogue

The dimmed house lights softly illuminated the stage in the auditorium. A lone podium stood stage left where a spotlight would soon shine. A large gray screen hung from the rafters, swaying just a touch from backstage fans that oscillated. An ever-increasing crowd gathered outside the auditorium doors. Excited conversations, as well as skeptical whispers, wafted through the air waiting to see the much-anticipated footage promoters promised would put the Bigfoot debate to rest once and for all.

Corrine sat fidgeting in a brightly lit dressing room. She dreaded the makeup process. She never liked wearing a lot of it to begin with, let alone adding what seemed like an extra half-inch of it to her face. Yet, she almost had too. Her light, alabaster skin called for it as protections from the intense stage lights she would have to endure for over an hour.

The makeup artist wanted to add a touch more base, but Corrine waved her off. Corrine asked the makeup woman to step out. She just wanted a moment alone to review her introduction and visualize herself walking out to the podium with poise and confidence.

A promoter advised that in order to make the most of her appearance, she should walk across the stage from the opposite side of where the podium stood. This act gave the audience time to applaud while allowing her to give a wave, smile at the audience, and bow gently before settling in behind the microphone to give her program.

"Ready?" came the stage manager's voice, popping her head in the dressing room to make sure Corrine was set to go.

Corrine pursed her lips and nodded. She had plenty of experience in public speaking. As a salesperson, she'd given many presentations let alone the sales workshops she had hosted or co-hosted. She had already given several private screenings (all participants signing nondisclosure forms until she made her news public) of her footage and presentation to a variety of experts over the last ten days.

Today marked her public debut. Word of her ordeal had spread like wildfire, even attracting the attention of national news and talk shows. Her new agent, Tim Brussard, was in negotiations with who would get the big interview with the woman who had definitive proof of Bigfoot and the story of how a group of them killed her colleagues out in the middle of an Oregon forest.

However, now, she was presenting at the Sasquatch Summit Conference just south of Seattle – no recording devices were allowed in the auditorium. This gathering was the biggest Sasquatch event concerning serious research and evidence into the mysterious beast. Scientists who believed in the possibility of the creature attended and held symposiums. Some of the toughest critics of the alleged creature participated in a variety of panel discussions. Bigfoot enthusiasts of renown (such as Sam Ashford in the past) contributed to discussions and held their own symposiums. The event also attracted plenty of science fiction writers, and vendors, as well as enthusiasts of other mysterious entities such as the Loch Ness Monster, Ogopogo, and others.

When word circulated about Corrine's story and her subsequent last-minute addition to the schedule, hotel availability dried up as well as the tickets to get in the room to see her presentation. The center hosting the event had to call in extra security. Registration skyrocketed, and press credential requests went from four to four hundred. Corrine's presence became an international story as journalists and reporters from all over the world descended on the scene.

"You'll be great," the stage director, a middle-aged woman, with a similar build as Corrine's said. She placed a hand on the small of Corrine's back to help guide her through the couple corridors they had to walk.

"Thanks," Corrine whispered.

The two entered into the backstage area.

"Look at me for a moment," the woman said, motioning Corrine to look at her eyes. "I'll receive word when to send you out. First, you'll be introduced, listen for the applause and then you're on."

Corrine nodded. She felt as if a bubble began to surround her, the enormity of the moment beginning to mount. "Okay. I'll wait for your cue."

Corrine lost her sense of time. Her vision became a tunnel as she stared at the podium on the other side of the stage. She stood perfectly still, repeating her introductory remarks over and over again in her mind. It went well in visualization. *Now if I could get feeling back in my legs, I might just pull this off.*

"You're on," the stage manager said and gave Corrine the push she needed to wake up her body.

As soon as Corrine hit the stage, the applause exploded. She knew she had to look out into the audience, smile, wave, and nod. If she simply bee-lined across the stage without looking out into the crowd, it would have sent the wrong signal, a sign of nervousness or worse, suspicion and doubt about her claims. Holding her poise, standing tall, she flashed a relaxed grin, gave two small waves to no one and mouthed thank you a couple times. She didn't want to look at anyone in particular but couldn't help but notice the entire audience standing up.

Corrine stopped just short of the podium, turned fully to the audience, smiled, and gave a short bow as the applause continued to roar. Taking her position behind the podium, she quickly smoothed out areas of her mostly blue dress with small fragmented patches of white scattered throughout; a simple thin black belt cinched her waist, accentuating her attractive curves. She grabbed the small black handheld presentation clicker off the top shelf of the lectern and positioned it in her right palm.

"Thank you for this honor," she said with a polite, humble voice. She eyed the packed room of seven hundred and fifty plus people, flashed another engaging smile but this time shifted her body cueing the audience she was about to begin. The room went quiet in seconds.

"The footage, pictures, and stories I have to share are all true, and tragic. Yet at the same time what I offer to you is nothing short of fascinating and enlightening for the entire scientific community and enthusiasts who have kept an open mind about this once elusive creature we know as Sasquatch."

With that, she pressed a button on her clicker and up came an image of three shadowy figures just beyond a row of trees. The audience clamored with surprise before erupting into applause.

"Before I continue, I just want everyone to know that even though what I have to show and offer you tonight is of considerable scientific importance… this was no ordinary expedition." She paused as true emotion gushed over her. A flash memory of snuggling with Chet, gazing into his eyes, touching his mouth with her finger, made her smile for a moment. "We lost 15 people that night and early morning, including a man who proved his innocence as a wrongly convicted murderer, Chet Daniels. If it wasn't for Chet, and the others who I will talk about in more detail, I would not be here tonight to show you the world's best footage and pictures that I believe, unequivocally proves the existence of Bigfoot once and for all."

She clicked her controller and brought up an image of the Sasquatch structures. The audience gasped at the large formations, the bent trees, the tiered lean-to/fan-like configuration, the way newer trees stacked over older ones. Corrine gave the audience a moment to soak it all in. She then clicked her remote to reveal a few more images of the site that she had captured on her phone.

Corrine continued. "When we first encountered this scene, that we dubbed Squatchtopia, we froze. No one moved. We stared in awe at what stood before us." Corrine stayed silent for a few seconds as the photographs displayed various angles of the structures. "I have some video, so you can better understand what I mean." She clicked the controller and video that Pete shot rolled. She didn't look at it. She'd seen it, lived it. Instead, Corrine watched the faces of the people witnessing the footage: dropped jaws, wide eyes that didn't blink, frozen expressions. Her eyes scanned the crowd in a casual manner front to back, stopping at different people whose appearances grabbed her attention.

The stadium seating design of the auditorium brought her eyes eventually into a sightline with the spotlights on the second tier, which impaired her field of view. As her glance crossed its way towards the back, something caught her eye. Rather than wince and look away because of the bright lights, she stared harder. She squinted hoping to focus better. For a moment, she could have sworn she saw Chet's silhouette. The figure stood leaning against one of the room's entrance doors just like Chet would lean against a tree as he gazed off into the woods. Same build, height, it had to be him - she felt assured it was him, but... how? She looked with more intensity, but the figure stood directly under one of the key lights shining on her. She adjusted her hand to shield the light, desperate to confirm her instinct. *That's Chet.* She knew it.

"Chet?" she accidentally chirped, her mic picking up her voice and sending her one-word query into the audience. Eyes shifted toward her. She noticed. With a meek smile, she apologized, said her emotions got in the way and encouraged the audience to watch the remaining minute left on the video. When all their eyes shifted back to the screen, she immediately looked back to the rear of the room. The figure was gone. An emotion of sadness cascaded over her. She wanted to run off the stage and call out his name. She couldn't, not now. Then an odd thought came to her and in a strange way, it comforted her. Chet had often said the only way he could lead a normal life, was if he simply disappeared and started fresh. She wondered if he may have somehow escaped, been given some bizarre reprieve by the beasts. She didn't really know, wasn't even positive it was him she saw. She hoped it was.

The video stopped. A moment of silence ensued. She caught herself staring off into the distance, cleared her mind, stood straight, smiled. "Stunning stuff huh... well, it was really just the start of some terrifying things to come."